ADVANCE PRAISE FOR *N*
FURTHER FROM

"In crisp, forthright prose, Christopher Evans's c...
compassionate collection of stories documents a present (and
near future) that is both utterly bizarre and ambiguously hope-
ful. This is exactly what we need to be reading."

—Carleigh Baker, author of Rogers Writers' Trust
Fiction Prize finalist *Bad Endings*

"Christopher Evans's stories fracture the mundane to reveal a
bedrock of absurdity. Like Donald Barthelme, Evans brandishes
humour in the face of reality, both defamiliarizing and helping
us see more clearly the familiar emotional lives of his characters. These stories will make you laugh—until you notice your
reflection peeking out between the pages."

—John Elizabeth Stintzi,
author of *Vanishing Monuments* and *Junebat*

"Evans's stories are littered with characters who are under the
impression they are normal people. They are horribly, tragically
mistaken...a perfect depiction of human nature. These stories
are hilarious, strange, and touching. At their root, they are an
exploration of the deep sadness of modern existence, which can
only be conveyed through an equally deep humour."

—Jen Neale, author of Rogers Writers' Trust
Fiction Prize finalist *Land Mammals and Sea Creatures*

"The stories in *Nothing Could Be Further from the Truth* draw readers into tiny worlds where the unreal combines seamlessly with the everyday. Written with humour and grace, Christopher Evans's characters are thrown into situations that grow absurd and out of proportion, amplifying their failures and faults and exposing the truth of modern life. This is a wonderful collection."

—Michael Melgaard, author of *Pallbearing*

"Uncanny in their capture of the anxiety of our times, these stories buzz with urgency, sting with humour, and probe a beguiling dream state: the absurdity and audacity of being human."

—Nancy Lee, author of VanCity Book Prize winner *The Age*

"The stories in *Nothing Could Be Further from the Truth* jangle with quiet urgency as their discontented protagonists grope for connection with each other and yearn for some small measure of fulfillment. Christopher Evans is so good at finding hilarity in the hopelessness, and cultivating tenderness for his flawed and fumbling characters."

—Jessica Westhead,
author of *And Also Sharks* and *Things Not to Do*

"This is a wonderful collection from a sure-footed writer with a great ear for dialogue. Meticulously observed, the stories illustrate how ordinary life often thrums with mysterious, elusive truths just waiting to be grasped, if only we are brave enough."

—*Foreword Reviews*

NOTHING COULD BE FURTHER FROM THE TRUTH

STORIES

CHRISTOPHER EVANS

Published in Canada in 2022 and the USA in 2022 by House of Anansi Press Inc.
www.houseofanansi.com

House of Anansi Press is committed to protecting our natural environment. This book is made of material from well-managed FSC®-certified forests, recycled materials, and other controlled sources.

House of Anansi Press is a Global Certified Accessible™ (GCA by Benetech) publisher. The ebook version of this book meets stringent accessibility standards and is available to students and readers with print disabilities.

26 25 24 23 22   1 2 3 4 5

Library and Archives Canada Cataloguing in Publication
Title: Nothing could be further from the truth : stories / Christopher Evans.
Names: Evans, Christopher (Author of Nothing could be further from the truth), author.
Identifiers: Canadiana (print) 20210273240 | Canadiana (ebook) 20210279478 | ISBN 9781487010331 (softcover) | ISBN 9781487010348 (EPUB)
Classification: LCC PS8609.V3353 N68 2022 | DDC C813/.6—dc23

Cover design: Based on the original by Andy Verboom and Kailee Wakeman
Text design: Alysia Shewchuk
Typesetting: Lucia Kim

House of Anansi Press respectfully acknowledges that the land on which we operate is the Traditional Territory of many Nations, including the Anishinabeg, the Wendat, and the Haudenosaunee. It is also the Treaty Lands of the Mississaugas of the Credit.

With the participation of the Government of Canada
Avec la participation du gouvernement du Canada |

We acknowledge for their financial support of our publishing program the Canada Council for the Arts, the Ontario Arts Council, and the Government of Canada.

Printed and bound in Canada

FSC
www.fsc.org
MIX
Paper from
responsible sources
FSC® C103567

To my grandfather, Lloyd Main,
who always knew I'd pick up a pen.

Contents

Always Hungry, Always Poor

I'M STANDING HALFWAY DOWN the block, smoking a cigarette, when I see the coyotes. I know the landlords know I smoke, and they've never said anything about it, but sometimes the wife landlord does this shallow cough thing when she sees me, and I'm never sure if she's being passive-aggressive or just has a scratchy throat, so I always move down the sidewalk to in front of that house that's never finished being built. This is the first time I've seen coyotes up close, and I'm surprised that I can identify them right away and don't just think they are regular skinny dogs. There are three of them, padding down the middle of the street in a V formation. They hear me exhale and stop, and the one at the top of the V—the leader, probably, because it's the thickest and has the least chunks missing from its ears—seems to sort of motion at me with its head, like *join us, friend*, so I snuff out my smoke and drop the butt in a shrub.

At a respectable distance, I follow them, back up the street, past the house. The coyotes move together like a tricycle, skirting the halos of the streetlamps, so I try to do the same, try to stay in the dark. Not that there is anyone around to see us anyway. It's that point in the season where the province has been on fire for weeks and the air is dense and clammy and everyone is ready for summer to be over. Most evenings, my landlords like to sit together out front and drink retsina, but tonight I can see the flicker of their pirated Balkan soap opera through the front window, which I'm glad about because they would definitely have something to say. A few times, after you left with Flossy, they invited me up from the basement to sit and listen to them talk. They both have this way of expressing things in the negative that's almost funny—they can't admit that the lawn looks good, just less hideous and patchy than before. The husband landlord travels for work a lot. When I asked about a recent trip, he said that Singapore was a dystopian hellscape, a living nightmare of concrete and glass and steel. I asked about eating and he conceded that the food wasn't awful.

The wife landlord has a bit of the darkness, too. The power went out a few weeks back, and when she and I came outside from our respective suites to see what was happening, there was a hydro worker harnessed to one of the utility poles. The wife started to yell at him about what was she going to do with all these cutlets going off in the fridge? The worker said that the outage wasn't him, that nothing he was doing had anything to do with the power grid, which just made the wife say terrible things, like how she hoped each member of his family died by choking on birthday cake. I just watched. After a few minutes of being berated, the worker climbed down and left. Later, the internet said there was an accident a few blocks away that cut electricity to the whole neighbourhood. I told the wife what I'd learned, but she just waved me off like I was talking craziness. The power was only out for forty minutes, so I'm sure the pork was fine.

The four of us weave through the playground and start across the elementary school field. People get so worked up about coyotes in the city, but I think it's nice. With all the construction all the time, something needs to take care of the rats, anyway. And it's not like they're dangerous like wolves or bears, just happy wild dogs with pointy ears. The coyotes' tails hardly move as they trot. I try walking bouncy through the grass like they do and start to feel better about myself and how I fit into the world, but then their scrawny legs make me remember that time we were hanging out with your friends from school and everyone was talking about bodies and the awesome variety of shapes available to humans. I didn't know how to fit myself into the conversation, so I made a joke about how my default physique was like that grade school experiment where kids stick toothpicks in an avocado pit and try to grow it on the windowsill—a spherical torso with stick-thin limbs. Everyone laughed, but then you lifted up the front of my shirt and poked where my belly pudges over the waist of my shorts and said I was missing the point of the conversation, which also seemed to miss the point of the conversation, I thought. Everyone got kind of quiet after that, and I wasn't sure which way I should be embarrassed. Later, you said you were trying to shame me into accepting myself.

I think the landlords were surprised that I stayed after you moved out. If they had the choice, I bet they would have chosen you to stay and me to go, even though I don't challenge them on anything and you have so many boundaries and opinions. Which is one of the things I like best about you, how you stand up for what you believe in. On Monday, I ran into the husband landlord on the sidewalk as he was getting home from work, late. There was an accident in the tunnel, traffic backed up for kilometres. *What kind of barbaric, backwater society relies on holes dug in the ground for transportation*, he asked. And I sort of knew what he meant. But then he said some racist things about Chinese people. If you were there, you would have said something, for sure—threatened to move out or report him on social media — but all I did was make my face look confused, like I didn't understand. After you yelled at him, the husband landlord would have probably respected you even more than before, and later, you would've given me shit about not reacting and reminded me that I don't have a well-defined belief system, just a bunch of stuff I'm hung-up about, and that having hang-ups isn't the same as having an interesting personality. You'd have said that feigning confusion is a trick I use to avoid problems, not to mention a sign of my privilege. But I don't know if that is really true because, sometimes, it's not a trick. Sometimes, I really don't get it, like why you insisted that Flossy come with you, even though she was my cat for years before you and I even met.

At the entrance to an alley, all three coyotes pause and look back at me. Their tongues loll out like they're panting, but they don't make any sound. One of them yawns, and I yawn, too. I wonder what it would be like to pet them, if their fur feels the same as a normal dog's. Do you know why Flossy's name is Flossy? It's because when she was little, her whiskers sort of drooped down like used dental floss. The name didn't just happen. I was a good cat dad, and I made a choice to call her that. You probably don't even know.

The coyote leader gives me a look like *hurry up, pal,* so I make my pace a little faster. I remember, when we were divvying up the stuff, you asked who should get the duvet and I just kept shrugging. You got mad and said it's like I'm never in a rush to join my own life, that I can never fully engage in living. That's why you are all snug somewhere and I'm on the floor in a sleeping bag I had to borrow from my brother.

But, look, I am participating now — embarking on an adventure in cross-species community-building. The coyotes' fur glows orange under the streetlamp. I feel nice again, in my body, like the atmosphere is the exact same temperature as me. Maybe this can be my life now — I will leave the basement behind and sleep in the cemetery with the coyotes and write about the experience and someone will publish it. You'll see how interesting I can be, and not through avoidance or fear or befuddlement but because I am alive and doing something special in the world. I'll turn this following into a kind of leadership. I'm proud that the animals have chosen me. I wonder if they already knew I would be there or if they would have waited until I came outside.

The breeze picks up a little; I get the smell of lavender from someone's backyard, then a whiff of garbage. The flanking coyotes spread to either side of the alley and snuffle around the recycle bins and trash cans. One of them disappears through the gap in a fence, then reappears a couple of metres down. I kind of want another cigarette—to celebrate my new canine friends—but the flame might spook them. Instead, I slowly raise my arms from my sides and up into the air, walk as my grandest self. I practise making my legs like springs, bounce on the balls of my feet. Somewhere above me, the moon glows behind the smoke.

Farther up the alley, something rustles behind a bank of black garbage bags and the leader's ears perk up even higher. The other two stop, then the one of the back coyotes darts behind the bags. There's the crinkling of plastic and a screech and a little tinkling sound. The coyote emerges from behind the trash with something large and limp in its mouth, something with a bell around its neck that briefly catches the light. It jogs over to join the other back coyote and then the two of them trot ahead, while the leader stays still. I take a step towards it. The leader yips—just once, but the sound arrests me, so I stop again. It turns in the direction the others have gone, but before it goes, it looks back at me and seems to shake its head like *we were wrong about you, guy, you are not the one for us.*

While it disappears into the smoke, I let my arms drift back down to my sides. I dig the cigarettes out of my pocket and have one on the walk home, careful to steer clear of the streetlamps. It's too quiet now, and my legs feel like wood.

Back at the house, the front steps are empty, but I can still hear the TV through the screen door. I sit down on the stair where I would sit if the landlords were outside and listen for a while. I try to keep up, but the show is hard to follow — there's jazzy music and a laugh track and what sounds like several characters crying all at once. The husband landlord finally says something, but it's in their language. The wife landlord laughs in her mean way, then sighs and answers in English, *Well, maybe it won't be as horrible as last year.*

Of This, We Were Certain

WE WOKE TO THE sound of a car door slamming. Those of us who were quick to rise made it to the windows in time to see the station wagon's tail lights moving away from the house in the dark. The bolder among us opened our bedroom doors and crept down the stairs as far as the landing before Father's voice strained from somewhere below to get back to bed, which everyone grudgingly did.

In the morning, Father called out again, inviting us all to the living room, where he sat slumped in the chair with the recurring pattern of owls and cornucopias, now dragged to the centre of the room. As we trickled in, he silenced our queries with a slow shake of the head and motioned us towards the couch and surrounding floor. Once everyone was accounted for, he spoke. "Your mother's left again."

Father closed his eyes and weathered the ensuing wave of exclamations, letting our reedy cries crash over him, as his fingers knit together and his knuckles went white. After we'd exhausted ourselves, he relaxed his hands and tossed a ring of keys to Myrna, the eldest at sixteen, and told her that she would have to take the remaining eight of us to school in two batches using the Pinto. We groaned, for we all hated Father's car, which smelled of gasoline and unfiltered cigarettes, and one of us asked wouldn't he need the car for work? Father shook his head again and told Mitch to call the school and tell them that some of us would be late. Father stood. "There's eggs in the fridge."

He shuffled out, first from the room, then from the house, heading towards the woodshed. Our voices mingled with the tinny echo of the screen door clashing against the frame.

Despite our commotion, this was not unfamiliar territory. We soon galvanized. Papers and pencil cases were stuffed into backpacks, a fistful of crunchies thrown towards the cat's bowl, the triplets goaded into shirts by Susan, employing Mother's long-established pattern for quick identification — Simon in green, Teddy in blue, Willy in red — while Myrna solemnly fried up a carton of eggs and Mitch spun a story for the school secretary. We took turns eating from the skillet, and after Myrna had left with the triplets and Charlotte in the Pinto, Hugh Jr. and I tried to pick nine decent-looking pears from the tree out front but only found six.

At lunchtime, we reconvened on the tetherball court. Susan, resourceful Susan, had traded her pear for a nectarine and the nectarine for a jelly sandwich, which she tore into chunks and distributed. As we chewed, we discussed the logistics of getting home and possible dinner plans and, eventually, our own private theories about what had happened. Mitch said that a few days before, Mother had suddenly hung up the phone when he'd walked into the kitchen. Myrna said she'd seen Mother leaning against the fence just the previous day, having a long conversation with the mailman, and you know what that means. Some of us made noises like we understood while others just stared. Poor Charlotte piped in. "The pretty angels took Mama away."

We were all used to such things from Charlotte and uniformly nodded until she beamed and went off to shout and kick at the tetherballs. The bell rang a minute later, and we parted company.

At home, Father remained reclusive, his presence known only by the occasional cigarette flicked from the darkness of the shed to smoulder in the dirt outside. Mitch and Susan got the triplets into the tub while Myrna fried up some ground chuck from the freezer, dumped in a can of mushroom soup and a box of Readi-Noodles and let Charlotte stir, cooing and grinning into the steaming pot. Once we ate, Myrna and I switched off reading stories to Hugh Jr. and the triplets until they fell asleep. The rest of us drifted off to bed when we saw fit.

We awoke the next morning to a half bottle of Canadian Club on the floor outside Father's closed bedroom door and again no station wagon in the driveway. Susan sold the leftover whiskey to the McVie brothers for ten dollars and used the money to buy a case of canned chili from the MegaSave and a couple loaves of bread and some potatoes. At dinner, we ate like kings.

By the third day, we still hadn't seen Father and were only able to identify that he'd been in the house at all by the mess left in and around the toilet. We again congregated on the tetherball court to discuss our fates. Mrs. Jacoby called us a gang and told us to disperse.

The next day was Saturday. We slept late, then sat around the living room in our pyjamas eating fried pears on buttered bread. With not a word from Mother, and Father now a ghost, we were all in agreement that this time was different. Even Charlotte understood, probably. She kept kneeling on the hearth, twisting to look up the chimney in case the angels were there, until Myrna made her sit still.

We began to question what would happen to us. Mitch said we should form a band and leave town. Susan said that was stupid and threw the rest of her bread into the fireplace.

The triplets got weepy and Hugh Jr. started yipping and punching at the headrest of the armchair and the pitch of the conversation got darker and darker until I couldn't stand it anymore and stood, spraying crumbs onto the rug. "They're idiots and I hope they both die. We're better off alone."

As I stood before my eight brothers and sisters, all fell silent. One by one they nodded, the truth finally spoken.

OUT OF MOTHER'S ABSENCE and Father's detachment, new household structures evolved. We developed routines and rarely deviated from them. We kept to our studies during the week and, on weekends, threw ourselves into a bottle drive that had us pushing the wheelbarrow door-to-door, collecting empties from our neighbours to cash in at the recycle depot. All conflicts were dealt with through a panel of our sibling peers. When Hugh Jr. ate the bologna out of Charlotte's sandwich and replaced it with millipedes, we decided that he was to either eat a millipede a day for the next month or become Charlotte's permanent schoolyard bodyguard. He sulked but didn't dispute the decision.

Our specific skills were honed. Mitch, eloquent Mitch, would speak on our behalf whenever an adult demanded attention of us. The triplets made the cat their baby and never let its bowl run empty. Charlotte, it turned out, could find any missing thing and disappeared at the news of a lost button only to emerge with it in minutes, dusty but ecstatic. Hugh Jr. poured his energy into bike rides to the dump, returning with glitchy radios or broken dollhouses, which I would repair and Susan would hawk at the junk shop and then transform the money into food, which Myrna would cook up and serve hot.

Hauled by Myrna, responsible Myrna, we'd arrive at school in parts but become again a collective at recess and lunch. So comfortable had we become with only each other's company that the other kids — even the McVies — began to shy away. We didn't care. Our grades had stabilized or, in some cases, improved. Mitch and Susan dominated at tetherball. When Charlotte bolted across the soccer field to holler at the geese gathered at the swampy end, Hugh Jr. would dutifully trail behind and wipe the mud from her shins. Mrs. Jacoby still watched us sidelong but otherwise held her tongue.

Father became less vaporous and could occasionally be seen indoors, sitting at the kitchen table in front of a cup of black coffee. He now had no more authority and offered no more input than the cat. He seemed to allow himself the luxury of silence, for which everyone was grateful. The sole responsibility he took was to split logs and stack the wood under the porch. Myrna began to leave a plate for him in the fridge after mealtimes, and sometimes he would sit by the hearth so Charlotte could scrape a plastic comb across his head, chattering at him in the same way she did her dolls. "Daddy has such nice hairs, what a pretty Daddy."

One day, after ferrying Mitch and the triplets back to the house, Myrna picked the rest of us up at school and drove us to the junk shop so Susan could pawn a mandolin Hugh Jr. had found in a ditch, which I'd polished and re-strung. With the fifteen dollars Susan got, we bought a family pack of pork cutlets, some day-old rolls, and the cheapest bag of apples and returned home to find the station wagon in the driveway. Mitch sat speechless on the porch. One of us asked what the heck was going on in there? He just shook his head and pointed to the open door.

In the living room, Father sat at one end of the couch, smiling tepidly, while Mother sat at the other, the triplets spread across her ample lap. The three boys talked excitedly over one another while Mother nodded. The rest of us stood stunned, except for Charlotte, who ran to the fireplace and scooched right in over the charred logs until she was touching the sooty back wall, her eyes moving incredulously up the chimney, then back to Mother. As Mitch came to cluster with us in the doorway, Mother looked up, then shushed the triplets and spoke. "Can someone put the kettle on?"

We turned inwards, our eyes roving from sibling to sibling, while we waited for someone to make a move, each too aware of the others' proximity. Myrna broke first. "Susan sold your curling iron."

Then Susan. "Mitch lied to Principal Holmes."

Then Mitch. "Hugh Jr. has been peeing in the sink."

Then everyone. "Myrna broke your Crock-Pot."

"Charlotte wiped boogers on the curtains."

"Teddy and Willy put Simon in the dryer."

Fingers flew and Mother's mouth pinched and Father got that distant look again and the sound rose and rose, and I slipped out between the bodies, from the house, across the yard to the pear tree. I jumped up to grab a thick branch and bounced and shook until unripe pears thudded down into the grass. I bunched them in my shirt and carried them to the driveway.

I dumped the pears onto the gravel at my feet, picked out a good, hard one and let it fly. It left a dent in the fake wood panelling of the wagon's driver door, aligned with where Mother's knees would be. I picked out another and threw again. And again and again, in a slow circle around the car, gathering the pears that had ricocheted away to throw again. The noise from inside the house faltered, then moved outside to resume from the porch. My eight brothers and sisters leaned over the railing and yelled my name over and over, and I threw and threw until the headlights cracked.

Nora, at the Cinema

NORA ARCHED HER BACK and drew her arms behind her, letting her hands trail along the shrubs that lined the path as she walked. Face tilted skyward, she closed her eyes and let the late-morning light turn her lids into little orange sunbursts. Her splayed fingers danced across the junipers, fresh green sprigs that sprung up to tickle her palms. As she neared Peter's house, the tickle became an itch, and the itch became an ache, and the ache travelled up her arms and forced its way down into her chest. Her heart pummelled her ribcage, began to surge with—

Nothing. Nora's heart didn't surge with anything, didn't alter its clockwork rhythm at all. Really, she was just walking with her arms out, at an angle that wasn't very comfortable. On some level, she knew there was nothing particularly meaningful or emotionally complex about the gesture. She knew it and hated that she knew it. And they might not even be junipers; they could be cedars or some other plant she'd never heard of. She'd have to google "coniferous bush" later. Nora wished it was raining or at least misty or something.

Peter's door was not just unlocked but slightly ajar. No reason for her to knock, no possibility for a poignant lovers' reunion on the porch. She shoved the door open, crossed the threshold over a toppled stack of motocross magazines, and went down the hall to the living room.

He was in much the same position as she'd left him last night—back against the couch's armrest, knees angled up, controller in hand. Peter still hadn't shaved. But the living room window cast him in a mellow light that was pleasing, the red tint in his dark beard appearing like embers, lightning-caught brush fires in a dense forest. She wanted to drape him in red-and-black flannel, fit him with a rugged knitted cap, pose him in front of a log cabin, steadfast hero of the frontier she knew him to be.

Peter ripped off a languid, damp-sounding fart. From across the room, she could see his nostrils flare as he sniffed and frowned. It took a few seconds for the waft to reach her. "Jesus, Pete." She fanned her hand in front of her nose.

Peter's eyes flicked up to Nora and back to the screen. "Yeah, sorry." His fingers continued to jab at the controller. "It's that chili. You just get up?"

"No, I—wait, did you not notice that I went home? Have you been here all night?"

Peter leaned towards the screen, staring intently, shouted something unintelligible, and dropped the controller to the floor. "I can sleep whenever." He stuck his pinkie in his ear, then balled something off the tip and flicked it. "What's up?"

Nora pointed to her purse, still on the couch a few inches from his feet. "My work keys."

Peter looked uncomprehendingly at the bag for moment, then back up to her and nodded. "Yeah, cool." He reached for the controller.

OUTSIDE, NORA SAT on the steps and pulled out her phone, sent separate messages to her parents: "Hey Mumma! thinking about u! call me XOX." "Hi Dad! Hope you're doing better! BBQ soon!? PORK=FORK 😊." She rubbed at her ears—still faintly bluish from the birthday earrings Peter had given her—then gingerly slipped in her earbuds. Pristine multi-harmonied folk rock filled her head. Back on the path, she absently patted the shrubs, their touch already meaningless, and pictured herself in soft focus, imagined how Sofia Coppola would light her.

Out on the main drag, she glanced at her reflection in the shop windows, craving a suggestion of her own profile, how she would appear to those looking out from the inside. How did her hair move when she walked? Should she use an authoritative stride or something more demure? To get an accurate picture was impossible. Sometimes, Nora wished that she didn't have to present as a person at all but as an image of an aloe plant or a baby wallaby. An aloe plant never worried that its body was a misshapen sack. A wallaby couldn't be expected to act as an intermediary in its parents' divorce, probably. Being a human was awful.

In front of Shelter, a homewares store, she stopped. There were rumours that the shop had replaced an actual shelter, but Nora was too new to the neighbourhood to confirm and, anyway, it was hard to care when the window display was so ideal in its starkness—white paint and raw wood, air plants suspended in teardrop-shaped holders, throw pillow with the word "womb" cross-stitched on it, framed oil painting of John Waters. Nora went inside.

The scent in the store—bergamot, maybe?—was the smell she wanted for her home, for herself. All the products seemed to be of the same genial, calming palette. The hand-painted appetizer plates fit in the cup of her hand, the bottles of sarsaparilla bitters had carved toppers that looked like gnarled roots. Nora wanted all of it—the colours and smell and the music in her ear—to fuse together into a lozenge that would never melt completely on her tongue.

Was it possible to actively develop synesthesia? She'd have to google that, too.

There was a wall of little wooden shelves meant for growing herbs. She picked up a price tag, then let it fall away when she realized it was almost as much as a student loan payment. Peter had built a beautiful herb garden out of a recycled pallet for his previous girlfriend. He'd shown Nora a picture of it a few years back, when they first got together, and said he'd make one for her. Not that she would have anywhere to put it if he ever did, not in her tiny apartment, with all her roommates' ugly crap everywhere. There'd be loads of room if she moved into Peter's place, but he hadn't yet asked. Nora took a picture of herself standing in front of a display of artisanal jarred asparagus, then left the store.

Further down the sidewalk, she approached Golden & Nest, the store where Peter had bought the earrings. It had been so touching that he'd remembered her birthday — let alone given her something, even if it wasn't wrapped — that she'd cried a bit, then felt embarrassed. The earrings were made in Paris — simple studs, spade-shaped, sterling with jade enamel. To match her eyes, Peter said. Nora's eyes were hazel but under the right conditions sometimes seemed to have green flecks, so she could see what he meant. She put them in, and Peter said she looked so pretty. After the dinner he ordered, after the cuddling and sex, while he snored beside her, Nora watched a documentary series on Netflix about chefs in France and was shocked at how labour-intensive croissants were. She fell asleep with his hand on her belly, a close-to-perfect evening.

A few mornings later, though, Nora woke to her ears throbbing. In the mirror, her lobes looked dark, bruised almost, except the holes, which were inflamed. She called Peter right away.

"Those fuckers," he said, yawning. "That was like forty bucks!" He didn't know where the receipt was but told her where he'd gotten them so she would know where to complain.

At the store, the woman behind the desk seemed to suggest Nora's ears were too sweaty.

"But look," Nora said, "the enamel's gone all cloudy, too, and kind of melted. It wasn't like that before."

"You must have worn them in the shower," the woman said.

"No, no, I haven't showered since I got them."

The woman grimaced. "You haven't bathed in four days?"

"It's too dry this time of year!" Nora pushed back her sleeve to show her chapped elbow as proof of the weather's relentlessness.

The woman simultaneously shook her head, shrugged, and exhaled, then said that they didn't do refunds but that she would contact the manager — who was away — to contact the jewellery-maker in Paris. They would let Nora know.

That had been weeks ago. Nora had emailed twice, to find out what was happening, with no reply. She passed the shop without stopping but tried to look sidelong through the window to see who was behind the desk. She couldn't tell and didn't want to risk entering in case it was the same woman again. Maybe they couldn't check their email for some reason. At the crosswalk, waiting for the light to change, Nora found their Facebook page and politely requested an update.

WHEN SHE REACHED WORK, Nora paused, let herself be framed by the coffee shop's doorway. She removed her earbuds and shook her hair out. She visualized the traffic behind her as an indistinct blur, like she was the centre of a tilt-shift photograph.

"Your shift starts at eleven." Her boss, Celeste, clomped towards her. "That means on the floor *by* eleven." Celeste held her watch out for Nora to see.

How would Nora's life be different if she'd been named Celeste? How would people's perceptions of her — her perception of herself — be different? Nora was a name for quirky girls, not a name the planets orbited. She didn't want to be a quirky girl, not really. She'd certainly be able to rise to the sophistication a name like Celeste required, definitely better than actual Celeste, who just wore pleated khakis all the time and looked like she cut her own hair, and not in a good way.

Her co-workers weren't much better. Each of them had a *thing*, something beyond and above work that their lives hinged on, something that locked Nora out. Shay and her research work in dyad symmetry, Alex always on about how enriching it was to build community wells in Sierra Leone. They were pleasant enough—nice, really—but supporting cast, at best, closer to the foreground than they ought to be. Also, Nora suspected they hated her and, during her worst spirals, lost sleep over what she assumed they said behind her back. They weren't very nice people, she decided. D-listers. Cruel.

The day dragged. Nora made flat whites and plated spelt scones. She carried used cups to the dish bin, carried the bin to the dishwasher, brought clean cups back to the counter. She voluntarily took out a bag of garbage and messaged Peter while standing in an alley that smelled like stale piss. "You are the rarest of delicacies. I am hungry for you." Nora wiped coffee grounds off the counter and adjusted her apron. She told Alex that she liked his glasses even though she didn't. An old man leaned too close and said, "Nothing brightens a face like a sunny smile. You should try that." And she did. She bent her lips over gritted teeth. She wiped sugar off the condiment station. Shay asked her what ever happened with the earrings, and Nora said it was all good. On the lid of the staff toilet, she sat and scrolled through her photos, buoyed a bit by how acceptable she looked in the Shelter picture, thankful that her ears were hidden under her hair. She sent it out for the world to see. Golden & Nest didn't respond to her Facebook message, but she could see that they'd viewed it. Nora sopped cream off the floor under a table. Her phone vibrated in her pocket and she crouched behind the counter to check it, but it was just a reminder that she'd used ninety percent of her data plan for the month. Should she message Peter again? Maybe she could re-send the same message, make it look like a technical error, remind him she was waiting. Nora folded napkins into tight squares to jam under the base of the tables so they wouldn't wobble. No one acknowledged her asparagus post and her parents didn't message her back. Golden & Nest posted a photo of their new line of essential oils to Instagram, and Nora "liked" it, then hated herself. She wiped and poured and smiled and wiped.

On her break, Nora sat on a bus stop bench down the block, ate the quinoa salad she'd made, and tried to start reading a novel. By the first page, she could tell the book would be dense with meaning. Why couldn't Alex or Shay or Celeste use the right words, say the perfect thing? It was like no one ever thought about what they were going to say before they said it. The salad was bland. The recipe had called for kalamata olives, which she didn't have and which cost seven dollars a jar. Her phone buzzed, and she put the book and salad down. She grinned when she saw it was a message from Peter, then slumped as she read it: "How hungry are you? LOL!!!" and a too-close photo of what might have been pubic hair and a testicle.

Was this what it felt like to be the most important person in another's world? Nora wondered if there was an alternate way to be needed by someone. No, wait, she didn't wonder; she fucking knew. Maybe she should foster a rescue cat. That would be nice, a tabby kitten that would curl up under her chin, maybe lick salt from the corners of her eyes when she cried. She could learn to crochet, make it little pajamas. Goddamnit, why couldn't Peter have just dealt with the earrings himself. They were supposed to be a gift. And why spades? She didn't play cards. Nora didn't respond to him, instead stabbed out a series of tweets: "@goldenandnest this is not how to treat a customer! #servicecounts" "why no return on bad products @goldenandnest?" "@goldenandnest #scamartists #blackears #boycott" She took a picture of her toxic lobes, and sent that, too. She closed the book without marking the page and picked the cherry tomatoes out of her salad, emptied the rest into the trash can. Her phone buzzed on the bench beside her: "@norathegreat92 *U*R*BLOCKED*""

Nora's break was over. Back at work, she tied her apron tight enough to leave a mark.

LATE IN THE AFTERNOON, Cardigan came in.

He walked over to a table and put down a stack of books to claim it, walked towards the counter, then rushed back to the table to sit and scribble something in a notebook. It looked like he was whispering to himself, but Nora couldn't be sure.

Cardigan ordered coffee almost daily, and Nora had somehow never spoken to him — didn't know his actual name — though she was aware that they were both aware of each other's presence. Cardigan always carried the kinds of books Nora wanted to want to read and had skin like milk dusted with paprika. While he was still hunched over his notebook, Nora slid past Shay to position herself behind the register.

Cardigan put down the notebook and shuffled to the counter. He looked up, then quickly back down to his hands and pushed some bills across the counter. "I'll have a large drip, medium roast, he said," he said.

"Did you just say 'he said'?" Nora asked. She squinted at him, tried to read his aura. Magenta, maybe?

"Er, no." Cardigan went paler still. "Probably not."

Nora studied him further. Today, he wore a T-shirt under his open sweater that read WASP SWAP. Was that a band that Nora should know about or just random cleverness? She thought for a moment, then leaned forward like a conspirator. "She slid his change across the counter," she said quietly, and did. "Room for cream, she asked, or non-dairy substitute?"

He took a sharp intake of breath, and his eyes flicked uncertainly between his hands and Nora's face. "Yes, thank you, he said," Cardigan said. "Soy." He cleared his throat. "He couldn't help but notice that the coins formed a glittering path between them."

Nora swallowed, too, hard. "She saw the same," she said, "that the gulf between them had suddenly been bridged."

"As he swept up his change, their skin was briefly introduced." With that, Cardigan's index finger darted out to run awkwardly down the length of Nora's pinkie.

Nora did not pull her hand away. "His touch electrified her." She knew it was a cliché as soon as she said it, but God, yes, she really did shiver, actually felt a shot charge up her arms, a tingle on her elbows. She hooked her hair over her ear, needed him to see the extent of her damage. Cardigan watched but didn't shudder with revulsion, didn't cringe or gasp. His glow intensified, outlined him like a gentle astigmatism.

Shay approached Nora and tried to reach past her to grab something under the register. "Sorry, Nora, I just need to—"

Nora and Cardigan held up their palms in parallel to silence and ward off Shay's nonsense. Shay blurred and faded to the background, as she was meant to. Nora stepped out from behind the counter.

"In that moment, everything they'd ever suspected about themselves was proven true." She moved closer to him and reached out her hand. Around them, the customers' idiot chatter became strings and acoustic strumming that swelled and swelled, a sound with a soothing, autumnal hue.

Cardigan took her hand in his. "Giddy in their new-found freedom—"

"—they withdrew themselves from the shackles of responsibility." In the hidden recess of their joined palms, she could feel their fate lines converging. "Their debts were paid."

Side by side, they stepped through the doorway and out onto the sidewalk, where the setting sun cast them in a bright, crystalline light. The store collapsed at their backs, mortar and stir sticks and cinnamon liquefying to flow down the storm drain. Nora's hair exploded into brilliance, radiated heat, threw purple sparks to burn the city down around them. Her lobes pinkened, perfect as twin kitten noses. The loose snags of Cardigan's cardigan detached and floated free to halo them like fireflies, and his freckles organized themselves into stars and anchors. Nora and Cardigan spoke in unison: "Their hearts heaved and roared, united in a sustained crescendo that lasted beyond all that could be understood." Neither of them farted, and no one felt ashamed. From the adjacent rack, bicycles became sentient and unlocked one another, rolled into the distance in pairs and healthy polyamorous triads, bells chiming. "Their souls sprouted wildflowers." They stared into each other's eyes and then past, into the deepest reservoir of their collective humanity. The green glass of the city melted and pooled, repaved the streets to complement her eyes, shimmered like the reflecting pool at the Eiffel Tower might. "At last and forever, they were one." Nora's apron rose from her waist, folded itself into an origami swan, flew above to dip and soar, to breathe in smoke and exhale the most innocuous of clouds.

I Don't Think So

W E GOT HIGH AND followed people in Marnie's old Plymouth. It was 1991. Her big sister let her have the car when it was too embarrassing to drive anymore. The rear seat was slung so low you needed help to get out, and the fabric that lined the roof back there had peeled off so it bubbled down like a veil in an opium den.

The car we were tailing was some kind of sedan, grey or maybe blue. I couldn't tell because I was wearing my sunglasses with the red lenses. The lenses turned all the blues and greens and greys into charred blood clots and the whites and pinks and yellows into electric magma. The blacks stayed black. It was summertime, hot and cruel.

The sedan was driven by an older couple — button-down suburbanites — which enraged Marnie, who I hadn't slept with yet and might never. Marnie hated the establishment and all their trappings — vests, dental care, expensive cheeses. She thought that anyone who made better choices than she did should fuck off and die. Actually die.

We followed the couple out of the parking lot at Town & Country Mall and up the Old Island Highway, away from the city. Marnie plugged in her Sonic Youth *Goo* cassette and, when the intro to "Kool Thing" came on, cranked up the stereo — the already half-blown speakers translating the music into trebly shards of raw noise — and gunned it so we were right alongside them. As we smoked our cigarettes and stared them down, the woman rolled up her window — panicky, stricken — and mouthed either "What do you want?" or "One to two wands?" Marnie and I just laughed and drifted back behind them.

This continued through the outskirts, past the car dealerships and the mini-golf, and further from town, up the mountain. The man in the driver's seat kept turning around and looking at us. Eventually Marnie started to do the same — look back — and, after a while, turned the music down and said, "I think we're being followed." While she was distracted, the sedan faded off into the parking lot of a Bino's Family Restaurant, the driver's eyes a flash of relief in the mirror.

I looked in the sideview in time to see another crimson landboat — another Chrysler — looming on my side, some tinny squall from the Chrysler's stereo cutting through the wind that screamed through our open windows. There was a girl in the driver's seat and a boy riding shotgun — in sunglasses, like us. Their cigarettes hung slack, ashes jetting behind them to pile in the back seat. I leaned out the window and shouted, "One to two wands?" They laughed and their car dropped behind ours. Marnie smacked the dashboard and said, "Those callous fucks." Sometimes, Marnie was the wrong kind of too much.

At the stoplight by the abandoned waterslides, they pulled up next to us and the driver, the girl, said, "You're in the wrong car." She was right. I got out, left my door hanging open, and crawled across her lap to sit between the two of them. Marnie swore bloody revenge and turned off, the passenger door slamming back into the frame. We continued up the highway.

They were siblings and blond. I didn't know their music, some kind of European brutalism with horns. I asked the girl if we could start dating now, but she just smirked and threw her cigarette out the window into the dry grass. I asked if I could kiss her, and she said, "No." Her brother said I could kiss him, and I did but didn't like it. We drove through sleepy shitkicker towns until the angry lava sky began to darken, our lungs swelling with acrid haze.

A maroon shape scuttled into the road and the girl swerved to hit it. It thumped and winged past — inert eyes, spattered teeth. I asked if I could take off my sunglasses and lie down for a bit, but the brother said, "No." He lit another cigarette with something oily inside. The girl kept checking her rearview and said, "I think we're being followed." Headlights backlit the cabin. Our faces were red, red, red.

At the stoplight by the burnt-out motel, a sedan pulled alongside us, blue or maybe green, radio cranked to a moderate volume — AM Gold. My parents.

My mother leaned out the window. "You're in the wrong car." I got out over the brother's lap and tried to climb in between my mother and father. My father hiked his thumb. "Back seat, Squirt."

The Chrysler peeled off to the left, birds flipped through the windows, and we kept going, up the highway, up the mountain. My father reached back, yanked the sunglasses from my face and sent them spiralling into the night. "Do up your belt." My mother handed back an afghan she'd been knitting — needles still tucked in her hair — and a glass of warm milk. Amid the blackness, under roof fabric that didn't sag, I lay down across the seat to a lullaby of buttercream vocals and airbrushed guitar and slept like my eighteen years had never even happened, or ever would again.

Cakewalk

RICHARD STOOD IN FRONT of a large, framed photograph, trying to find himself. He scanned the first row. There he was, with the rest of the kindergarteners, just to the left of the little engraved plaque on the bottom of the frame that read "1981," grinning in his powder-blue turtleneck and corduroys, the rest of the school spread out behind him like a fan across the soccer field. Stepping over to the 1982 photo, Richard again found himself easily, just a little further from the front, in a Superman T-shirt, hair cut to the shape of a bowl. He walked past the next few photos, picking himself out—a little deeper into the crowd each year, slight variations on the same haircut—until he came to 1988. Grade Seven. Only eight years ago, but it felt like forever.

His brain filled in the names as his eyes moved from face to face: Brian, Nicole, Sandy, Mike H., Mike S., Jennifer. He remembered posing for that last photograph because he'd stood behind Stephanie Bolano and Susan Pants and could see their bra straps through the fabric of their blouses. Yup, there were Stephanie and Sue, arms across each other's shoulders, hands over mouths to stifle giggles. Richard leaned in closer to the picture and held up his hand to block out the fluorescent glare against the glass. Tonight was the first time he'd seen the photo. It hadn't been printed and hung until after he'd moved on to junior high. Was that part of his arm showing just past Stephanie? Had he ducked down for some reason? He appeared not to be there at all.

He walked away from the photos, along the deserted second-floor hallway, past the darkened Principal's Office and silent administrative desk, towards the stairs to the main floor and the rising hum of voices. He let his hand trail along the corkboards on the wall as he moved, fingers snagging on staples and crinkling hand-shaped paper turkeys. One came unstuck and floated to the floor. Richard turned back and picked it up. The turkey's eye was off-centre, closer to its neck than its beak, and it didn't have legs. He shoved the turkey in his pocket and continued down the stairs.

He wandered the halls looking for his nephew, Connor, who had bolted within the first two minutes of being in the school, a clump of prize tickets tight in his grimy little fist. Richard waded through the hordes of children, a stampede of little feet making the floor rumble. Their shrillness was intense, all of them screaming for more tickets. Had he been this loud? Richard didn't think so.

IN THE GYMNASIUM, a long hand-painted banner hung above the pull-out bleachers: "Hazelwood Elementary Community Fall Fair 1996 + Science Fair." He walked up and down the makeshift aisles, past the shoebox dioramas and baking soda volcanoes, until he came to the Grade Threes' area and found Connor's project. It appeared to be titled "Raccoons Ar Friends?" and consisted of dozens of pictures cut out from old issues of *National Geographic* and sloppy hand-printed factoids about raccoons glued to a tri-folded piece of cardboard. Even from a distance, Richard could tell it was a shoddy job; one of the raccoons was a badger and two more of the pictures clearly showed red pandas. Typical Connor. The children were encouraged to stand by their science projects, to answer questions and receive patronizing comments from the adults, but Connor was AWOL. Richard's own third-grade Science Fair project had been about garter snakes, its centrepiece — an intact snake skeleton — gingerly placed in a protective glass box lined with black velvet. He stood guard over his project and answered only informed questions about garter snakes. He chose his *National Geographic* cut-outs carefully.

The Fall Fair side of the gym was a riot of activity,

separated from the Science Fair by a line of folding chairs. A parent-and-child three-legged race was on, uneven pairs falling heavily to thin pads lining the floor. High-jump mats had been pushed into one corner, where the Grade Seven boys performed piledrivers and tried to suplex each other. A line-up for the beanbag-toss station snaked along the wall, all the way to the bake-sale ladies. A few more folding chairs had been set up as an eating area, next to a table with a chafing dish full of limp pink hot dogs floating in murky water and buns still in their bags. Parents sat and commiserated. He became acutely aware that there were no other twenty-year-olds in the mix; Richard was alone in a sea of kids and old people. The whole huge room thudded with hollow noise. Connor was nowhere to be seen.

BACK IN THE HALLWAY, Richard spotted Mrs. Kaser, his fourth-grade teacher. On his year-end report card, she'd written "Ricky rarely answers question in class, but when he does his responses are thoughtful and clear. Ricky is a kind boy." He'd taped the report to the fridge, where it had remained for several years until it fell off and slid underneath. Mrs. Kaser had hugged him once after class, on a day when Shana Adams had called him "Rich-tard" in front of the whole room after he'd refused to share his coloured pencils with her. He remembered melting into the safety of that hug, breathing in her dense, floral smell.

Mrs. Kaser stood in a cluster of parents. Richard hovered on the periphery and tugged nervously at his wallet chain. He had almost reached out to pull on the sleeve of her sweater when the crowd broke. "Hi, Mrs. Kaser."

She smiled and nodded. "Well hello, young man." She waved to someone over his shoulder.

"Richard Belford, from Grade Four." Richard moved his head to try and stay in her line of vision. "You remember me?"

Mrs. Kaser continued to nod. "Of course. Yes! And what are you up to these days?" She called to someone further down the hall, "Hey, Connie! Better make that a double!" She gave a thumbs-up and laughed and turned her eyes back to Richard. "So, college then?" She gave him a once-over. "Or just finishing high school?"

"Oh. No, I graduated a few years ago. Just working right now. Video store, uh, management. Well, assistant management." Richard felt himself straighten up. "Just a workin' man now. Probably get my own place soon."

Mrs. Kaser patted his arm with one of her heavily ringed hands. "Well, that's just terrific, just great." She dropped her hand and started to move past him, her arms already spread to embrace someone else. "You'll have to excuse me, dear. It was very nice to speak with you again, David."

RICHARD LET THE DOOR slam behind him as he headed out into the damp night air. He walked to the cement alcove along the side of the building across from the tether-ball court — an architectural defect, its original purpose long-forgotten. Richard leaned against the wall and closed his eyes, breathing deeply, as the sounds from inside melted away. He could feel the concrete against his back, cold and hard through his shirt and jacket.

"You're Ricky Belford."

Richard turned to the voice. It belonged to a girl with bleached-out hair who pointed at him with an unlit cigarette. "You were in my sister's year, yeah? Tamara? Tamara Armstrong?"

Richard felt some parts of his body go tense and rigid while others went slack and weak. He leaned heavily into the wall and let it support his weight. What percentage of his waking hours had been spent thinking about Tamara? Thirty-five percent? Fifty? Richard swivelled his head around. "Is she here? Your sister?"

The girl snorted. "Fuck, no. She took off to Vancouver right after grad. Said we were holding her back." She lit her smoke and held the pack out to him. "Like she's the cat's ass."

"Totally," he said, without commitment, and slid a cigarette out of the package. The girl flicked her lighter and lit his smoke. Menthol—gross, but also good. "So, you're... Becky?"

"Wow, you remembered. I'm impressed." Becky leaned in closer. "So, Ricky Belford, what are you even doing here? Handing in a late assignment?" She might have winked.

"My oldest sister's kid goes here now. I'm supposed to be watching him, but he took off." Richard shrugged. "He's kind of a turd."

Becky laughed and shot smoke from her nostrils. "That's funny. I remember how you were funny."

That surprised him. He couldn't imagine how someone two grades behind him remembered him at all, let alone as funny, which he wasn't. He studied Becky; she looked a lot like her older sister, if he squinted and imagined her with darker hair.

Becky scanned the parking lot and tetherball court, then stepped closer. She pulled down the zipper of her jacket, to reveal a low-slung top underneath. A mickey poked out of the top of her bra. "Want a taste?"

Richard exhaled and stepped back. "Uh, I don't . . . um. Aren't you still in high school?" He narrowed his eyes again, so his vision blurred. "Well—"

Becky tugged the bottle out of her bra and waggled it at him. "Graduating this year."

"Oh, good. That's okay." Richard chuckled to himself, glad it was too dark for her to see his cheeks turn red. He moved back towards her. He accepted the bottle and took a slug, wincing as the liquor seared his throat. Becky took the bottle from him and belted it back without so much as a blink. She dropped her cigarette to the ground—the butt smeared with pink lipstick—and let it smoulder until Richard crushed it with his heel. They passed the liquor back and forth a few times before Richard held up his palm and said, "I'm supposed to be babysitting."

Becky laughed—a sharp, hard blast. "Fuck that. You're coming with me."

RICHARD HAD GONE ALL the way from kindergarten to Grade Twelve with Tamara and spoken probably twenty words to her in that time. He still remembered her valedictory speech—not the wording, exactly, but the sentiment. It was a kiss-off; Tamara made it clear that she made it to where she was—high marks, top of the pecking order—all on her own merit. She'd succeeded not because of her teachers and peers but despite them. Her shitty attitude had made her even sexier, in Richard's estimation.

Becky Armstrong had the same raspy voice as her sister, and probably the same hair colour before the bleach, and maybe a similar shape under her winter coat, and the same shit attitude. Richard knew the resemblance to Tamara stopped there, but he still let her pull him through the crowd, her hand small in his, brushing past students and parents and teachers. They went into the classroom with the apple bob station and quickly out again, into the room with the pop bottle ring-toss and out, scanned the face-painting tables without stopping. Richard half-heartedly searched the faces for Connor's. He studied the corkboards in case any of his own artwork—like that awesome dragon picture he'd done in Grade Six—had been preserved. It hadn't.

Becky seemed to know a lot of people, a lot of teenage girls anyway. She clung fiercely to Richard's arm as they approached and giggled or whispered into Becky's ear and gave Richard knowing looks. The alcohol muddied him, left him with little to do but nod and smile. As they waded through, Becky told him about the nail salon she would open after she finished school, which she would call *Beckeez*. Richard said that sounded great and told her to let him know if she ever needed a doorman or a bouncer. He tried to picture himself at an Armstrong family dinner, Becky at his side, while Tamara sent him regretful looks from across a table piled with food. He would announce the promotion he'd have gotten at Gung-Ho Video—full-time hours, full manager—and everyone would be so impressed. Maybe the sisters would even fight over him, each one's hair in the other's fist.

Outside a classroom blaring with music, Becky stopped and turned to Richard. She placed one hand flat against his chest and reached up to tuck a lock of hair behind his ear. He craned his face towards her, head tilted to the side.

Becky pushed him back with one hand, while drawing his hip closer with the other. She laughed loudly and looked at something out of the corner of her eye. "Oh my God, Ricky," she said. "That is sooo funny!" Her hand slid across his lower back and, as she turned her face away from him, it briefly dipped down the waist of his jeans. The touch against his bare skin echoed after it was over.

"Oh, hello there, Troy." Becky regarded a sullen looking boy who watched them from a few feet away. "I didn't expect to see you here." The boy had on a leathery 8-Ball jacket and lines shaved into the side of his hair. Becky pushed Richard towards him.

"Troy, do you know Ricky?" She pulled Richard back closer. "Probably you don't. He's older."

"Hey." Richard held his hand out, and the boy took it, one iron squeeze.

"Pff," Troy said.

Becky laughed again, as though someone had said something hilarious. "Anyway, I'd love to shoot the shit with you, Troy, but Ricky here is going to win me a cake." She reached both arms around Richard's torso and hugged. "Right, Ricky?"

Richard nodded dumbly and allowed himself to be dragged into the classroom. Becky dug her hand into his jacket pocket, pulled out the rest of Connor's tickets, handed three to the woman seated at the CD player, and stuck the remaining ones in her own pocket. She propelled Richard forward.

Richard stood on a piece of construction paper painted with a number twelve, one of a series laid out in a circle in the centre of the room. Becky was quickly enveloped by a trio of girls at the edge of the room, their eyes lifting occasionally to assess him. Troy leaned in the doorway and smirked. Richard was several heads taller and a decade older than the rest of his competition. On the number directly in front of him, a child with pigtails hugged a stuffed owl. The music started—Salt-N-Pepa's "Whatta Man." Richard began to move.

He stepped haltingly from number to number, watching his feet, the papers too close for his long legs. A hand reached out and removed one of the sheets. The music stopped. Richard stood on sixteen. One child left the circle. The music resumed. Richard lurched. The chain from his wallet slapped his thigh.

As he circled the room, Richard's eyes darted from place to place. This had been his classroom once—Grade Five. He passed Becky, still in the huddle of girls. He passed Troy, who might have mouthed "Fuck yourself" at him. He passed the table of decorated, homemade cakes. He passed the narrowed eyes and disapproving head-shakes of parents and teachers. A number was yanked from the circle and the music stopped. Richard stood on eight, the child behind him bumped into the back of his legs and was left stranded. The music resumed.

On his next pass, Richard saw that Becky had left her girlfriends and moved closer to the door. Next round, he saw her in a whispered conversation with Troy. When he circled around again, they were gone. The room was nearly empty. Richard decided it would be worse to leave in the middle of a walk than to stay. If he jumped ship now, it would be like an admission that he didn't belong there.

He looked around the circle to size up his four remaining competitors. A kid two children back, with a face painted like some kind of animal, stuck his tongue out at Richard. Connor. The music started.

Richard glanced back at his nephew. "What are you supposed to be? A rat?"

"I'm a raccoon, duh."

Numbers were pulled, the children departed. Soon it was just Richard and Connor pacing around a single piece of paper. Richard looked down, watching his and Connor's feet. The initial buzz of the liquor became an angry throb behind his ears. The music played on and on and on until it didn't. Richard stomped his foot down on the number four.

"You're a jerk, Uncle Rick!" Connor fled from the room. Someone behind Richard booed, but he didn't turn around to see who.

HE WALKED DOWN THE hallway, a round cake on a cardboard tray in his arms, its icing an ugly swirl of purple and green. He went into each of the classrooms, back up the stairs to the quiet second floor, into the same gymnasium where he had sung "O Canada" and "God Save the Queen" so many times. He stepped over a pile of sawdust by the drinking fountain, a sure sign some hyped-up child had barfed there. Richard knew Becky was gone—probably sucking face with Troy somewhere—but kept an eye out for her, just in case. He briefly considered just giving the cake to his nephew, but what would Connor learn from that?

Richard leaned into the pushbar of the door and went out into the night air. The door slammed behind him. He carried the cake through the tetherball court and past the smokers' alcove until he came to the parking lot.

He placed the cake on the ground in the middle of the lot's entrance, where it was sure to be run over. Under the streetlight, he could see a smear of purple icing across the front of his jacket. He ran a finger through it and up to his mouth, leaving behind a taste of greasy sweetness and nicotine. As he jammed his hands into his pockets, he felt the turkey's paper feathers crunch under his knuckles. Richard retreated to stand in the gravel outside the streetlight's range and waited for a car to come or go.

Over the Coffee Table and
Down the Hall

I T HAPPENED DURING a fight, a big one. They'd each been
nestled into their respective ends of the couch, swaddled
in itchy, striped blankets, their breath producing little white
billows in the frigid air of the apartment. Brian had been
in the process of providing reasons why he shouldn't be
the one to call about the heat. His name wasn't on the
lease, so it was Meredith's apartment, really. Brian merely
lived there. He had never been properly introduced to the
landlord before, only nodded to him in the foyer. *And you
know how I get around strangers, don't you, Meredith? Have some
empathy for once.* Couldn't they just shell out for another
space heater or throw some plastic up over the windows
instead of suffering the indignity of placing a phone call?
Use some common sense, Meredith. Honestly.

A large part of Brian's skill lay in the fact that he appeared not to be fighting at all. The closer Meredith crept towards unhinged, the more logical and evasive Brian became. *Meredith, you can't expect me to be responsible for the weather.* The ease with which he explained away her feelings created in her a resentment so deep she was rendered mute. While her body stiffened with futile rage, Brian reclined deeper into the couch, feet crossed and propped on the coffee table. *Don't you think you're overreacting here, Mer? Just relax.*

Meredith stood and paced, ragged blanket draped across her shoulders. She closed her eyes to stem the flow of useless tears, but a steady stream continued to spill down her cheeks to dampen the neck of her sweater. She tugged surreptitiously where the wool chafed her skin. *Put on another sweater if that one's bothering you, obviously.* Meredith squeezed her eyes shut as tight as she could until she saw roving, milky impressions of the overhead light on the inside of her eyelids. With her hands clenched into powerless fists, she gulped in air and tried to control her breathing in order to release the accumulation of words dammed up inside of her. *Could you please have the decency to look at me when I'm talking to you, Meredith? You're being rude.*

It was here, at the apex of her frustration, that Meredith felt a ripple pulse through her body. It began in her chest and emanated outwards, into her stomach and limbs and head. She felt the blanket fall away, brushing the back of her calves on its descent. Meredith heard Brian gasp and opened her eyes to see a look of uncomprehending shock slapped across his face. She followed Brian's eyes, first up to the stuccoed ceiling, now just inches above her, then down to the scratchy blanket, heaped on the floor beneath her feet.

The two of them remained locked in this tableau for nearly a minute: Brian, mesmerized, anchored, bracketed by the paisley upholstery of the couch; Meredith, stunned and silent, backlit by the halogen lamp, a shadow puppet motionless in the air.

Meredith blinked and plummeted. Her shins jarred painfully into her knees as she landed, and she stumbled forward, knocking fronds off the desiccated fern next to the plywood-and-cinderblock bookshelf. Brian sat there, slack-jawed, as she picked herself up.

Brian's immobility endured, but his silence didn't. Did she have supernatural powers, dormant until her thirtieth year? Was she a ghost? Were they both ghosts? Had she had contact with radioactive material? Could the apartment be built on a burial ground? Had she allowed scientists to perform experiments on her? *Explain yourself.* The dam inside of her finally cracked and released all her words in a torrent that Brian shrunk away from, miraculously without comment.

Since her outburst, Brian had been uncharacteristically thoughtful and meek, rinsing his stubble out of the sink and trying to rub her feet. *There's nothing I wouldn't do for you.* He stared at her with a kind of quiet awe that Meredith found oppressive.

Meredith replayed each detail of the event in her head, every minute of every day since. Her own unspoken theory ran contrary to all of Brian's idiotically predictable science fiction and fantasy speculations. She remembered the rejection that had risen in her so intensely in the seconds before she floated. Meredith hadn't pulled herself towards the ceiling so much as she had propelled herself away from Brian and the shabby couch and the poorly insulated room and the unpaid student loans and the questionable future.

Mer, you know how much I love you, right? She supposed she loved Brian, too, or at least didn't not love him. But in that brief moment of suspension, dizzying as it was, Meredith felt a freedom she hadn't felt since she was a child sprinting headlong into the ocean's spray, a freedom she suspected Brian neither sought nor understood.

Her obsession now — that she would be unable to replicate the circumstances that led to the event, that she'd never again feel as free — heightened with each sign of Brian's new-found respect. *Don't worry about the recycling. Can I make you some tea?* As Brian's compliance grew and his arrogance diminished, Meredith feared that she was being pulled towards him and the life they would half-heartedly build together and further from her potential.

She knew that if he truly wanted to see her levitate or hover or fly or whatever it was, he should stop picking up his wet towel from the floor and washing dishes and bringing her almond croissants on her lunch break. If he reverted to his usual self—patronizing, ineffectual Brian—and provoked her with his thoughtlessness, he just might witness her float over their second-hand coffee table and down the hall, out through the wide kitchen window, past the stand of scraggly cedars outside, and up into the night sky.

Burrowing

I GUESS IT ALL started a few weeks after the business closed. I was starting to get real worried about Janine. Actually, if I'm honest, neither of us was doing too hot; just wandering around the house, drinking vodka-and-7s and eating hot dogs. Janine was up to a full pack of Matinée Menthols a day, and I was hitting the hot knives pretty hard. We were watching a lot of *Wheel*. But it was worse for her. She just took the whole thing so goddamned personal, y'know, like it was her fault the economy tanked and everyone went low-carb, got insecure about how fat they were and stopped eating muffins.

Anyway, we were sitting around in our bathrobes one night, about four hours deep into a Nature Channel marathon, when this documentary about burrow owls comes on. Janine totally perks up all of a sudden and starts jabbering about how they were all over the place when she was a kid and how come you don't see them anymore? She's telling me about how a family of them used to live under her Nana's porch out in Del Bonita and how she used to ride her bike down to see them all the time — right up until the tornado took the porch off in '86 — and how they have the coolest yellow eyes.

And then I remember how my cousin Mikey was talking about how his buddy Pete, down in Montana, had set up this animal sanctuary so he could get money from the government or something. When I tell Janine, she gets real excited and starts saying how we should go down there to see if he's got any owls and let's go tomorrow. And I'm like, sure, it's not like we've got anything better to do now that our business is in the shitter.

In the morning, I call Mikey, and next thing you know, we're in the Nissan and we're talking to the guy at the Sweetgrass border crossing and he's giving us directions and telling us that we should stop at his sister's restaurant in Starburst. So we do. We drive to Stacey's Place, and I order the Huevos Rancheros and Janine gets the Trucker's Breakfast. Janine's in a better mood than I've seen her in months, like she didn't even care that we were out driving around instead of watching *The Price Is Right*. Janine talks to the guard's sister, Stacey, and it turns out that she knows Pete, too, and yeah, he's got buttloads of owls down there. Janine nearly shits.

We get to Dumont and find Pete's property and meet Pete, who's this friendly old guy with an eye patch who used to bowl with cousin Mikey. Pete says he talked to Mikey and welcome to Montana and did we want to see the owls? Janine's so keyed up that she's shaking like our old washer. We follow Pete down this path to a big fenced-in area with a sign that says "Western Burrowing Owls" that Pete said he painted himself. Sure enough, there's the owls. There are piles of them, with brown feathers and weird, skinny legs, and they mostly just stand there until Janine freaks and some of them run off or go back into their holes. Pete has to tell her to slow down there, Miss.

We talk about the owls for a bit, and I ask Pete, if they're owls, how come they're out during the day and he says they're mostly daytime owls. Janine can't get enough of them, so after a while I take a walk with Pete and he shows me his porcupine and a deer with a limp. I ask if there's any way I could take a couple of owls off his hands. Pete says, well, he shouldn't, but to tell you the truth, he's only supposed to be caring for the injured animals and the owls are breeding like crazy and keep trying to move into the prairie dog habitat. So I make a deal.

Now we fast-forward a couple weeks: I've fixed up our fence, built some little perches, and punched a bunch of burrows into the yard with Mikey's fence-post driver. After the initial owl high, Janine had come down pretty hard—like worse than before she even started a business, which was supposed to be our answer to everything and look where that got us—and isn't paying attention to what I'm doing and barely goes out back anyway. I mean, there was nothing really back there except the picnic table and the grill and the shed, which was mostly just filled with muffin tins and totally infested with mice—basically a big dusty brown square with one ratty poplar, so why bother? Anyway, I tell Janine I gotta go help my dad drywall his basement and she just shrugs and rolls over, and I wish I knew how to just fix everything with words. But I don't, so I hop in the Nissan and fuck off.

I drive back down to Montana and hand Pete one hundred and fifty bucks, Canadian. He gives me six owls in two old rabbit cages, which he says I can keep. We load them in the back seat and Pete wishes me good luck and don't tell anybody, and then I'm driving back to Milk River with these little peckers behind me, hooting and beaking at the wire. Just before Coutts, I pull over and cover the cages with a sleeping bag and move them into the hatchback and hope like hell that it's Brenda or Marty at the border and not Ike or the Mendholson kid. Sure enough, it's Marty, and he says he was real sorry to hear about MuffinZone and do Janine and I want to come over Friday for some steaks? He doesn't even look in the hatch.

Back at home, I take the cages around back through the

side gate and then go in through the front door and Janine's in the kitchen making eggs, wearing my old sweatpants and that *Shrek II* T-shirt we won at the Multiplex in Lethbridge. I tell her I have a surprise and she says the eggs'll get cold, but I turn off the burner anyway and drag her outside through the screen door. I whip the sleeping bag off the cages and Janine completely loses her mind, jumping and crying, and the owls go nuts. We let them out of the cages and they go flapping and screeching across the yard and some go in the holes I made, so I'm totally stoked. We pull up a couple of lawn chairs from the front porch and have some drinks and watch the owls for the rest of the day. I can really see the appeal now—those little buggers are hilarious. That night I get the first hummer I've had in months, and in the morning, Janine's up and making muffins before I even roll out of bed.

The next couple weeks are awesome. I pick up a few shifts at Ray's Electric, so we have some money coming in again, and Janine cleans up around the house and starts making this scrapbook with feathers from the yard and cute internet stories, and I'd forgotten how foxy she looks in the sunshine. I mean, she was getting super pale there for a while from never getting out of bed. Sometimes the medication just doesn't do what it's supposed to, right? The owls have taken care of the mouse problem in the shed, which is great because neither of us liked going in there in case we got the Hantavirus from all the turds.

The owls are making lots of new burrows and seem pretty psyched to be there. The only problem is they don't ever sleep, and screech all night long. Forget what Pete said—daytime owls my ass. Fortunately, our bedroom's at the front of the house so we can't really hear them, and our only close neighbour is old Edna next door, who is basically a million years old and practically deaf.

But then 9:30 one night, someone is banging on our door, and it's this guy who says he's Edna's son, who I remember is some bigshot from Saskatoon who owns a bunch of Subways or some such shit. He says he's staying with Edna for a month while she recovers from cataract surgery and our owls are keeping him up and do we have a licence for them? I can't figure out how he knows that the screeching is coming from our yard, seeing as how the fence is wood and about eight feet high, so first I say what owls and then tell him that we do have a licence and I can see he doesn't believe me, but whatever. When I tell Janine about it, she gets hella nervous and we stay up half the night trying to keep the owls quiet, but it turns out you can't really shush owls. We tack some old camping blankets up to our side of the fence to make it more soundproof and it seems to do the trick because, a couple days later, we haven't heard from him again.

That Sunday is Canada Day, so Saturday night we have Mikey and his girlfriend Trish over for some BBQ and drinks. We hang out in the yard all afternoon and play lawn darts — away from the owls obviously — and Janine makes her wicked potato salad and Trish brings over this huge cake with a maple leaf on it. I buy the good smokies, and I'm sitting on the left side of the picnic table so I can flip them without getting up when Trish sits her ass down across from me and the table drops about a foot on that side. Not because Trish is heavy or anything but because the owls have been burrowing under the table and the whole ground gives way.

Anyway, I pitch forward right into the barbeque, and that's how I got this scar. The smokies go flying and Trish is screaming because she somehow gets wedged between the bench and the tabletop and the citronella candle falls over and gets hot wax all over her arm. Mikey's freaking, trying to pry her out, and the napkins are catching fire from the candle and starting to float around the yard. I can barely see anything because I got blood in my eye from bashing my forehead, so I yell for Janine to get the hose from the front tap. She panics and can't get the side gate open and tries to climb over it instead of just going through the house and falls, and I can hear her groaning on the other side. I tell Mikey to get some water, and he runs into the house right through the screen door, which breaks, and he gets these little mesh marks all over his nose and cheek, which is pretty funny later.

Meanwhile, I'm trying to stomp out the burning napkins before the grass catches, and Trish is just standing there like a dumbass, picking wax off her arm. Mikey comes back, looking all dazed with his face cut up, holding two coffee cups full of water — useless — that he dumps on the vinyl tablecloth, which is burning and melting, too. Janine manages to get the gate open and limps in with the hose — knees bleeding like crazy — and comes hustling over but steps in a burrow and falls flat on her face. While Trish is helping Janine up and I'm hosing down the last of the napkins, I hear someone calling from over the gate. I yell for them to let themselves in, thinking that someone must have called the fire department and how that's sweet response time.

But, turns out, it's not the fire department. It's animal control, which Edna's jerkoff son must've called. This chick is standing there in her white shirt and cargo shorts, with her net and clipboard, just staring while we're still running around and the owls are screeching like mad and everyone's bleeding, except for Trish who's just burnt.

The chick from Alberta Animal Services is named Ocean, which if you ask me is a pretty stupid name for someone who's probably never been west of the Rockies, and she's not impressed with the whole situation and tells us so in no uncertain terms. While Trish and Mikey take Janine over to Milk River Health, Ocean continues to chew me out for having endangered animals on the property and wants to know where I got them from. I tell her I bought them off some kid at the side of the road out in New Dayton and didn't know it was illegal and the kid looked like a real perv, so I was basically doing a public service. She rolls her eyes and tells me the owls have to go, irregardless, and how this whole thing is a total hassle. I ask what she's going to do with them, and Ocean says maybe the Calgary Zoo will take them or else she knows a guy named Pete down in Montana who runs this animal sanctuary, except taking animals over the border is a real headache with a lot of paperwork attached. I ask her if we could just keep them and she says no.

A couple days after all this goes down, me and Janine are sitting out back, drinking Jack-and-Cokes and staring at the yard, which looks even worse than before. I guess the owls really went to town on the burrowing because the ground is all uneven now and there's a big hole where the picnic table was. Janine's on crutches, with her ankle bandaged up pretty good, and she's even more depressed than she was before the owls, which means no more muffins or hummers for yours truly. I feel really bad about the whole thing, even though it's not my fault, and she looks so dejected, and I want her to be happy, like I *need* her to be happy, I can't even deal with the thought of her lying on our gross old bathmat again and crying, and I feel all shitty and helpless like a tiny baby who can't even move its arms or legs or do a single fucking thing to help anyone, and I can't be alone, I can't, I can't, I can't, I can't, and I just sort of blurt out maybe we should get married?

So, long story short, we're on our honeymoon, and that's what brings us to West Edmonton Mall, and thanks so much for asking! I just thought I'd nip in here to get Janine a surprise while she's trying on shoes, so how much are those lovebirds in the window, and do you know if they'll eat mice?

A Species of Setback

I.

In a fit of maternal concern, Charlene sat down and wrote two letters—one to her daughter, Samantha, and one to her daughter's now ex-husband. The letter to Roger had been easy. She thanked him for his years of service as a son-in-law, wished him well, and said that she hoped he'd still make the drive out from Kamloops in the summer to help her re-shingle her roof. The letter to her daughter proved difficult. Charlene danced around variations of *I just want you to be happy* but struggled to find wording that Samantha would not find insulting. In the end, she wrote that she'd enjoyed Samantha's recent stay and hoped she would return soon and included a cheque to help her start her new life as a single thirty-five-year-old in Vancouver.

She worried that even the cheque was a potential offence, so Charlene decided to drive into Creston to post the letters before she lost her nerve altogether.

She steered the truck down her winding driveway, the moon flashing yellow and full between the dark outline of the trees. Once she hit the main road, Charlene turned up the truck's cassette player and sang along to "Jet Airliner" in her high, wavering voice, the letters wedged between her thigh and the cracked vinyl seat.

At the edge of town, Charlene made a wide U-turn and pulled up onto the opposite shoulder, alongside the Canada Post box. While the truck idled, she rolled down her window and leaned out. This was the position Charlene held — one wrist facing skyward as she yanked the drawer open, the other facing the earth as she dropped the letters in, neck craned, squinting under the pale light of the street-lamp into the black mouth of the box — as the first one fell. The bird was small and brown and brushed her wrist on its descent. She swore and jerked back into the truck, then cautiously leaned out the window again to stare at the body in the gravel at the post box's base. A wren, one wing folded unnaturally beneath its back.

As she swung open her door to study the bird further, another thumped against the hood. Then another. In the forest around her, branches shuffled and creaked as more fell. A heavy *thunk* against the post box. She ducked into the truck and turned to look out the back window, up to the moon behind her, obscured now in a haze.

On the road, the going was slow. When the birds fell, they fell without grace, plummeting heavily to the pavement, grim silhouettes in her high beams, yellow beaks and white breasts flaring in the light. As ravens and swallows and flycatchers ricocheted off the roof and filled the flatbed, Charlene picked up speed, no longer trying to drive around the bodies but crunching forward towards home.

Just as she reached her driveway, something large and dark cracked the windshield. Charlene screamed and flailed at the wheel, sending the truck into the ditch, where it dipped before making an arc into the treeline. As she hung suspended by her belt in the cab, bodies continued to drum against the undercarriage and the cassette played on.

II.

Shortly after Sam had announced she was leaving him and going back to the Kootenays to live with her mother, a woman had offered Roger a smoke while they'd stood outside the conference centre waiting for taxis. He had thanked the woman—a sales rep for a pet food company he sometimes did business with—and eased one out of the pack. He'd turned down her offer for a light though and tucked the cigarette gingerly into his breast pocket before stepping into the cab alone. It didn't occur to him until he was in his kitchen—the cat mewing and weaving between his legs as he searched for a pack of matches—that the woman had likely been flirting with him. With this realization, the cigarette suddenly seemed sordid, an affront to the marriage he was still hoping to salvage, so Roger dropped it in a baggie and placed the baggie into an empty coffee tin high in the cupboard, as furtively as he'd hidden weed as a teenager.

Now, many months later, after he signed the last of the divorce paperwork, Roger poured himself two fingers of whiskey and brought the tin down from the cupboard. He carried the tumbler and the paper and the cigarette to the back porch and sat, the old rattan loveseat squeaking beneath him. He flipped again through the papers, yanked away all the little plastic tabs the lawyer had used to indicate where Roger should initial, and then—satisfied, unsatisfied—dropped the stack onto the seat next to him and lit the cigarette. The cat—Sam's cat, really—yowled from the kitchen, trapped on the wrong side of the screen door.

The cigarette was stale. It burned quickly, and the smoke felt thick in Roger's mouth. He took three slow drags before it became clear to him that he was going to throw up. He balanced the cigarette on the edge of the glass patio table and rushed inside while the cat rushed out. As Roger puked onto the bathroom floor just a few feet shy of the toilet, the cat leapt from the floor to the glass table and from the table to the loveseat, impassive as the cigarette dropped and the paperwork drifted down. She perched in the spot Roger had just vacated and chirruped softly. The neighbours' cat—a lean Siamese—squeezed through a gap in the fence and hunkered in the grass to watch.

The fire started small, then grew. It bloomed along the edge of one page, then moved quickly through the rest of the documents—Roger's and Samantha's names first browning, then burning—before licking at the leg of the loveseat. The cat hopped over the armrest, padded across the porch and down the steps to the yard as the loveseat began to crackle, hidden pillbugs and sacs of spiders' eggs popping and hissing in the heat. The fire spread out, across the porch, up the side of the house, towards the steps and the dry grass of the yard, as Roger retched and sobbed on the bathroom linoleum.

The cat sauntered over to the furthest edge of the yard and turned to watch the flames. Other cats filtered through and over the fence, squatted on their haunches in the grass, trilled their secret language. As the tumbler exploded and the liquor caught, the cat—Roger's cat, Sam's cat—licked at her paw. The plumes of smoke rose to blot out the moon.

III.

It began with an itch in the crease where Sam's leg met her body. Her hand moved sluggishly from the top of the duvet to beneath the covers and slid down the front of her pyjama pants, a fingernail jutting out to scratch at her inner thigh. She retracted her hand and tried to return to sleep.

The itching resumed. She rolled from her side to her back and jammed both hands down her pants, feeling for a tag or a wayward shard of potato chip. She felt another tickle on the tender back of her knee, then felt something scuttle across her stomach, just south of her belly button. She slapped at her lower body and reached out to turn on the little bedside lamp. In the light, a silverfish darted across the sheet, towards the gap between the bed and the wall. Sam clamped a hand to her mouth and screamed into it.

She scrambled from the bed and dropped her pants, kicking them off into a corner of the darkness. Standing in front of the full-length — now just in a saggy tank top and socks — she inspected herself from all angles in the lamp's dim glow, propped her legs up on an open drawer, peered back over her shoulder as she spread her cheeks slightly, her breath coming in short, sharp bursts. Sam shuddered as her hands roved over her thighs and calves, up under her top, and dug down below the elastic of her socks.

She flicked on the overhead light — a pair of fluorescent

tubes that hummed and cracked and lit the tiny suite in an ugly whiteness. The whole room convulsed with movement.

The floor at her feet was a writhing mass of silvery bodies, a desperate flash and leap of scales, like the cutthroat trout she'd seen in Goat River as a child. Everything on the floor, on the desk, on each flat surface, every freshly bought symbol of her new life, each memento from her old one, shifted as the silverfish tried to escape the glare. Papers fell, mounds of dirty laundry shuffled, a stack of lifestyle and cooking magazines near the door teetered and slid. On her dresser, an empty kale chip bag crinkled, a pale, inch-long body darting out, then retreating back inside. Sam's screams stuck in her throat.

She staggered back, tapered abdomens and twitching antennae crushed by the pads of her feet. Her hands could not stop moving, scratching at her torso, flying down to cover her groin. She careened into the window, the moon blinking at her as she flapped at the venetian blinds. Sam clamoured back onto the bed, upset the duvet and released another grey horde, which surged towards her to find shelter in the shade of her body.

Curled into a ball, Sam felt the silverfish wriggle beneath her, their tens of thousands of metallic limbs surfing her across the sheet, her head tapping lightly into the headboard. Eyes squeezed tight, she breathed into her forearm and wished she'd never come to the city, wished she'd stayed in the stifling warmth of her mother's kitchen. She wished even to have remained in Roger's tepid arms instead of being left to lurch atop a shimmering sea, alone.

A Dissection of Passion

SANCHÉ WAS THE GREATEST writer the country had ever produced, or so Murielle believed. She stood in a line that snaked from the library's entrance, across the square, and down the hill almost to the waterfront, waiting for a chance to meet the man. In her hands, Murielle carried two items: a book and a cake.

The book was one of her favourites of Sanché's, an early novel about a young man who splits himself in half to please two lovers. Murielle had read *A Dissection of Passion* at least once a year for the past dozen, her heart careening against her ribcage every time she reached the passage in which the protagonist cleaves his soul and leaves neatly wrapped halves in front of his lovers' houses. The cake was a humble thing: yellow sponge with a simple frosting of egg white, cane sugar, water, and vanilla bean, decorated with red berries in a spiral pattern, resting on a chipped blue plate.

She'd arrived at what she believed would be an early enough hour only to find many, many women—and a few romantic, bookish young men—already queued, each person carrying one or two books with Sanché's winsome face pictured on the back. Sanché was a prolific writer. In only one of the last twenty years—the year of the coup— had he failed to deliver a new title. However, since that year, books had become increasingly scarce in the country. Murielle had still managed to collect all of Sanché's, trading as many as five bags of the melons that grew rampant in her tiny yard to a shady dealer in the city's marketplace for a single book.

The day grew hot and the line moved slowly. In order to block the cake from the sun's rays, Murielle stood at an awkward angle. She used her book to fan away the wasps and hornets that tried to alight on the icing. As she stood sideways between the two silent, unsmiling women on either side of her, Murielle thought again about *A Dissection of Passion* and how Carlo, the young protagonist, has to appear to his lovers only in profile so they won't discover that his affection is shared.

JOSEF SANCHÉ HAD BEEN tricked. After months of cajoling, his agent—a florid-faced Finn named Hannuken—had finally convinced him to end a decade of self-imposed exile and return to his homeland for what had been described as a "Day of National Celebration of His Inestimable Talent." He'd flown on a large, modern airliner from his adopted city to Reykjavik, from Reykjavik to St. John's, from St. John's to Chicago, and from Chicago to Miami, where he was transferred to a rusty little four-seater, the tail of which was painted in the colours of his country. His escort on the flight from Miami to the capital was a grim, thin, high-ranking officer who sneered at Sanché over the top of his newspaper.

It was this man's presence and the headline of the newspaper he held—"The Lost Lamb Returns! Country's Greatest Export Pledges Support to Its Greatest Leader"—that made Sanché realize his agent had not been truthful. It was the pistol the man pointed at him, as the two of them strode across the tarmac, that made Sanché realize Hannuken—that pig bastard—had likely profited from the situation. And it was this man's hand, with its long, delicate fingers, as it slid the passport out of Sanché's blazer pocket and tucked it into the pocket of his own military tunic, that made Sanché realize that he would probably never be allowed to leave his country again.

And now, weeks later, as he sat hunched in the library with the same grim, old officer standing over his shoulder, an endless procession of dull-eyed citizens lined up before him, Sanché realized fully that he'd become a puppet of the regime he'd left behind.

AFTER SEVERAL HOURS, MURIELLE found herself at the foot of the library's wide steps, in front of a signboard that read "For Three Days Only, Our Prodigal Son, the Novelist Josef Sanché, Will Be Signing Books as a Gesture of Renewed Commitment to Our Great Country." Below the words was a badly copied and cropped photograph of the writer, taken many years before. In the picture, Sanché wore a tuxedo and sunglasses, his hair slicked like a wave crashing on the beach, his left hand holding a dark drink in a short glass, his right arm flung carelessly across the shoulders of someone who had disappeared out of the frame. It was a well-known photo. The figure clumsily cut from the picture was the country's former leader, a good friend of the writer, who'd been hanged in the same square in which Murielle now stood.

After another forty-five minutes and a slow march up the steps, Murielle found herself within a few paces of the signing desk. Sanché looked no less handsome in person— greyer, for sure, and a little heavier, but no less handsome. Murielle's heart thudded inside her chest.

Sanché signed the inside of a book for a woman at the front of the line. As he handed the book back to her, Sanché smiled. But as she turned away, Murielle saw the smile fade. He laid his pen down on the desk and massaged his hand, squeezing together the fingers and knuckles. Murielle could hear them crack. Behind Sanché stood two uniformed men, a young lieutenant to his left and a thin, older man to his right, whose insignia marked him as a general of some sort.

The next person in line, the unsmiling woman directly in front of Murielle, sprung suddenly forward towards the desk, speaking loudly and excitedly. The young lieutenant became startled, and his hands flapped and wrenched at his holster. The unsmiling woman screamed, causing the lieutenant to holler and brandish his pistol in further response. As Murielle stepped back and the woman screamed and the lieutenant hollered and Sanché winced, the older man, the general, swiftly commandeered the situation with a few quick movements. He cuffed his hand around the lieutenant's shoulder to calm his needless panic and guided the hand with the pistol back to the holster, then held up his palm to stop the woman's histrionics and brushed his fingers forward to move her back into line. Once both had obeyed, the general picked up the pen from the desk and held it out for Sanché to take.

Sanché looked ill. "May I please have a glass of water?"

"After," the general said, still holding out his hand. Sanché took the pen. The general reached across the desk and took the book from the woman at the head of the line and dropped it in front of Sanché with a *whump*. The writer flipped the book open, signed his name, and closed the cover. The general motioned for the woman to take the book and pointed to the exit.

Once the woman was gone, the general signalled for Murielle to approach the desk. Blushing, she held the cake out for Sanché to see. His eyes widened in surprise as they shifted between the cake and Murielle's face.

"Your books have meant so much to me," Murielle said. "I cannot tell you —"

"What is this?" The general's eyes narrowed.

Murielle turned to regard the older man. "It is a cake, General."

The general's long finger, quick as a palm snake, darted across his chest to point to the insignia on his opposite shoulder. "No, no, no." The finger tapped at a small icon of a grenade stitched below the chevrons of his armband.

"It is a cake, *Brigadier* General," Murielle said. "I baked it as a gift for Sanché, our country's greatest writer." She looked back down to the author, who beamed back at her from the desk. Sanché's hair looked even thicker than Murielle had imagined.

Sanché spoke: "How lovely! What a pleasant and unexpec —"

"This man? The greatest writer?" The brigadier general laughed with a sound more forceful than his slight chest would indicate. "Clearly, you have not studied the writings of our Great Leader. If you had, you would understand the folly of your statement." He clapped Sanché roundly on the shoulder and looked over at the young lieutenant, who eagerly began to laugh also. The brigadier general leaned over and laughed into Sanché's ear. Sanché issued a brief chuckle and looked down at his hands.

Once his laughter had subsided, the brigadier general continued: "All frivolity aside, you must believe this man to have a tremendous greed to think him desirous of such a gift. As we all know, the integrity of our homeland hinges on the distribution of wealth amongst its people." He slapped Sanché's shoulder again. "Surely, a man like this, a humble agent of culture, would want to see such fine cake shared with his compatriots. Is that not true, writer?"

Sanché did not raise his eyes. Murielle tried to will him to stand up and obliterate the old man with his fist, but Sanché did not. Instead, he spoke into his hands. "It is true; the cake must be shared. To do otherwise would be an insult to our Great Leader."

The brigadier general reached down and pulled a long, silver blade from his black boot. He handed the knife to the lieutenant, with instructions for the distribution of the cake. Murielle and Sanché could only watch in silence as the young lieutenant cut the cake into tiny slivers and walked the length of the line with Murielle's blue plate, passing pieces to the other book enthusiasts, who licked their fingers and celebrated their good fortune.

The lieutenant returned the empty plate to Murielle and wiped frosting from the corner of his mouth with the sleeve of his tunic. The brigadier general, smiling, waved Murielle to the desk. Sanché took *A Dissection of Passion* from her, scrawled something across the title page, and slid the book back across the desk, his eyes never once rising.

"Thank you." Murielle turned away.

As she retreated, she heard the brigadier general speak. "The both of you should be thankful for such small sacrifices. Long live our Great Leader."

MURIELLE TRUDGED HOME, the book clutched to her chest, and let the empty plate bump against her thigh and rain crumbs down to the dirt. She crept through her squat, government-built house, past the sagging sofa where her mother and her two boys slept in a tangled heap, past her narrow cot in the kitchen area, across the small porch, and out into the yard. She stepped through the riot of melon vines to the rain barrel and rinsed the plate, then dried it with the hem of her skirt and walked back into the house and placed it on the shelf where it belonged.

Murielle returned to the porch and lit the lamp. She

placed the novel on her lap and opened it to the title page, where Sanché had written:

Sanché

Disappointed, Murielle closed the book. She went back inside to the kitchen area, knelt down, and slid a shallow wooden box from beneath the cot. Murielle pried off the lid and sifted through the items inside—the last of her late husband's personal effects, God rest his soul. She pulled out a faded knit jersey, collected her knitting needles, and returned to the porch. With great care, she began to unravel the jersey, long spirals of green and grey yarn collecting at her feet. As she worked, Murielle thought again of Sanché, the only man to touch her soul since her husband had died, and how she would visit him again tomorrow. Perhaps the brigadier general would not be there. Perhaps Sanché would be less tired. Perhaps he would speak her name.

JOSEF SANCHÉ PACED his room at the Pacífico Grand Hotel, his heels clacking against the parquet floor. "Room" was maybe an exaggeration—it was a cell. Bars on all the windows, two armed sentries outside the door, two bowls of rice and beans delivered each day. The room had no phone, no television. He was permitted no visitors. Who would visit anyway? All his contemporaries had fled or been imprisoned or died under suspicious circumstances.

Shortly after he was returned from the library, Sanché's door had been again unlocked and opened to allow an ancient, nearly silent man — a barber — entrance. The barber sat the writer on a chair in the bathroom and trimmed his hair and eyebrows, speaking only to tell Sanché that he must have a haircut before the photograph was taken. The old man neglected to sweep up, leaving a pile of salt-and-pepper locks on the marble floor.

After the barber had gone, Sanché lay down on the bed and thought about the signing. That woman today with the cake and the pleasing hips, she had been kind. The people here were so different than when he had left the decade before — gaunt and worn, their eyes empty. That woman, though, she'd had a spark of compassion. No woman had baked for him in a very long time. Sanché ran his hand through his short hair, sprinkling small, wiry strands on to the pillow.

THE NEXT MORNING, MURIELLE stood in a line that snaked from the library's entrance, across the square, and down the hill almost to the waterfront, waiting for a chance to see the man again. In her arms, she carried two items: a book and a scarf.

The book was another of Sanché's best, a novel about a man who discovers his lover has been transformed into a jaguar by a bitter rival. Murielle kept her copy of *The Forbidden Heart* on the little shelf above her cot, and after her mother and sons were asleep, she would often re-read the passage in which the protagonist discovers that a jungle cat is stalking him and strips himself naked, waiting for it to pounce. It was a scene that made her body tremble. The scarf was a simple thing: green and grey stripes, woven together from the strands of her dead husband's jersey. There would likely be few occasions when the weather cooled enough to warrant it, but perhaps Sanché would take it with him back to Scandinavia, where Murielle understood the air was always clear and crisp.

After a few hours, Murielle again found herself within a few paces of the signing desk. Sanché looked more tired today, slumped in his chair in front of an open book. He scratched his name across the inside cover and handed the book back to the woman at the front of the line, offering the briefest of smiles. Sanché's hair had been cut, his Bohemian look all but gone. Again, the young lieutenant and lean brigadier general stood at his back.

As Murielle approached the desk, Sanché's worn face broke into a weak grin. The brigadier general's eyes narrowed, and the lieutenant drummed his fingers against his holster.

"I'm so pleased you've returned," Sanché said. "I was afraid I wouldn't get a chance to thank—"

"What is this?" The brigadier general's finger jutted out to indicate the scarf balled under Murielle's arm.

"It is a scarf, Brigadier General. A gift for Sanché, our country's greatest writer."

"Oh, what a generous—"

"This man?" The older man did not laugh. Instead his mouth spread into a thin and unpleasant smile. "No, no, no. There is only one person in this country deserving of such a gift, and it is certainly not this man." The brigadier general placed a slender hand on each of Sanché's shoulders and kneaded the flesh there. He looked over to the young lieutenant, who began to grin also. Sanché closed his eyes. "This man is but a servant of the arts, a simple man, a small man." He hunched down so his face was at the same level as Sanché's. "I am correct in saying so, am I not, writer?"

Sanché opened his eyes and stared again at his hands. "That is correct. Compared to our Great Leader, I am no one."

Murielle's heart sagged.

"Then it is agreed." The brigadier general clapped his hands once, sharply, and pointed to the scarf, which the young lieutenant snatched and stood awkwardly holding. The brigadier general leaned forward, took *The Forbidden Heart* from Murielle, leaving her arms empty, and placed it in front of Sanché. The writer flipped open the cover, wrote inside, and closed it.

Murielle took the book and looked up to see the brigadier general rubbing the wool of the scarf between his smooth fingers. "This will do nicely to protect our Great Leader's fine neck as he walks the beach at night, contemplating means to protect us from foreign tyranny."

MURIELLE TREKKED HOME, her book held fast to her chest. She crept through her house, past her slumbering family, and on to the porch. She lit the lamp and opened the book.

Josef Sanché

Murielle put down the book and picked up the lamp, carrying it across her yard with its choking tendrils of melon vine and into the small field beyond to search for Sanché's last gift. As Murielle walked, she thought again of *The Forbidden Heart* and about how Juan, the protagonist, and his love, in jaguar form, bed down together in the long grass after her identity is revealed.

IN EUROPE, JOSEF SANCHÉ had grown complacent and fat on cream and cured meats. The university where he taught brimmed with wealth, his students a bunch of spoiled, condescending children who thought little of his work and treated him as an exotic curiosity. He resented them all the more because he knew they were right to dismiss him. Sanché's last few novels had been terrible—he knew it, his agent knew it, his audiences in Europe and America knew it. It was only in his homeland, this strip of land surrounded by jungle and sea, with its isolated populace, slow-minded from years of hunger, that no one realized what a joke he'd become.

As if to further stress the sad comedy of his existence, Sanché had been returned to his cell to find a young man—a photographer's assistant—fussily dressing the space. The assistant set a typewriter on the table near the window and arranged the curtains so they let in the last of the day's light while obscuring the window's bars. The assistant suggested that, for the photograph, the Great Leader could be standing just over Sanché's shoulder, in front of the typewriter, allowing the impression that the great man was helping to guide the writer's work. It wasn't even Sanché's typewriter; his own machine had travelled with him all the way across the Atlantic, but he'd not seen it since disembarking the plane.

After the young man left, Sanché stood by the window and thought again of that woman with the scarf and the thick calves. He felt she was an ally. But an ally of what? He wished she could share his bed.

Sanché gave a short, hard laugh. "What does it matter anyway?" His voice echoed through the large room. It was only the bars that kept him from throwing open the window and dashing himself on the cobblestones below. He reached out and muddled the curtains, then laughed again at the futility of the gesture.

ON THE THIRD MORNING, Murielle stood in a line that snaked from the library's entrance, across the square, and down the hill almost to the waterfront, waiting for a chance to see the man one last time. In her arms she carried two items: a book and a small woven basket.

The book was one of Sanché's most recent, a novel about an older fisherman who discovers an underwater city populated by all the people he has ever lost — his parents, his friends, his lover from his younger years. *Five Fathoms of Desire* was not one of her favourites, but she wanted Sanché to see that she'd made some effort to follow his career in the time he'd been gone. The book had cost her three bags of melons. The basket was hastily made, woven from dried grass and palm. It rustled as she walked.

Murielle stood in front of the signing desk. Sanché looked ragged and despondent and didn't even look up until she was right in front of him. The cadaverous brigadier general and the dumb, young lieutenant stood behind him.

Haltingly, Sanché began to speak: "I must apologize a million times. I'm afraid... I'm no longer my—"

"What is this?" A smirk played across the brigadier general's lips.

"It is a gift for Josef Sanché, our country's greatest writer."

The brigadier general waved for the lieutenant to collect the basket and remove the lid. The young lieutenant yanked off the woven top, shouted something unintelligible, and replaced the lid. The older man rolled his eyes and snatched the basket, his hand swift as a rock sparrow. He plucked off the top. As he looked inside, his eyes first narrowed sharply, then relaxed. His smirk transformed into a wide grin.

He looked up at Murielle. "Your persistence has finally come to fruition. Yes, yes, yes, now here is a gift suitable for a man such as this." He laughed, long and loud, and looked over to the young lieutenant, who began to snicker uncertainly. The brigadier general's hand reached over and mussed Sanché's greying hair. He leaned close to the writer's ear. "Finally, this woman has captured your character." The brigadier general held out the basket so Sanché could look inside.

The basket contained a fat, pale scorpion, huddled to one corner, its tail poised to strike. The scorpion's pincers and back were decorated with a paste Murielle had made from the last of the red berries. A pattern of rough hearts dabbed on with a twig.

The brigadier general let loose another volley of laughter as he reached forward and patted Sanché's cheek playfully, an almost intimate gesture. "A fitting gift for you, yes? An insect?"

Murielle studied Sanché's lined, handsome face as it peered into the basket and shifted from bewilderment to thoughtfulness to delight. He looked up at Murielle and her heart thrummed so loudly she feared the men might hear it. Sanché began to join in the officers' laughter. "A more fitting symbol of my return there could not be." He held out his hand for Murielle's book.

As he opened it and readied his pen, he again looked up at her. "I never learned your name."

"Murielle."

"Murielle. Beautiful." He scratched across the inside cover, and then slid the book across the table. When she reached for it, her hand brushed the back of his for just a moment. As she walked away, she heard the men laughing anew.

MURIELLE FLOATED HOME. She bent to kiss her two sons and her mother on their foreheads, drifted past her cot and out to the porch, where she lit the lamp and sat, the book tight to her chest. She moved the lamp closer and opened the cover of *Five Fathoms of Desire*.

> *Murielle,*
> *I will carry your kindness with me always, from this moment to the grave. You have emboldened me with your wonderful gift.*
> *Josef*

Murielle's breathing became shallow and sharp. She quickly turned to the one passage in the book that she really was very fond of. Alejandro, the old protagonist, dives deep down to the underwater city and presses his hand to the dome that protects his loved ones inside. His lover, still in the flush of her youth, presses her hand against his from the other side. His breath leaves him and he floats up towards the surface and away from her. Despite the general poorness of the book, it was the most romantic scene Sanché had ever written.

Murielle blew out the lantern and stepped to the yard. She curled up on the ground, a melon for a pillow, and let her hand travel under her skirt. After her tremors subsided, she thanked the world for its beauty and fell asleep.

JOSEF SANCHÉ AGAIN WALKED the floor of his cell at the Pacífico Grand. He'd been escorted back to the hotel lobby by the brigadier general, a smirk still plastered to the old man's skeletal face, who'd handed him over to the two armed sentries who, in turn, escorted him to his room. On parting, the brigadier general had said, "Enjoy your precious gift," and had laughed again. The woven basket had twitched in Sanché's hand.

As Sanché paced from one end of the room to the other — from the locked door to the barred windows — he continually passed the desk. Eventually, he allowed his steps to slow and then cease, and he sat down in the chair in front of the fraudulent typewriter. He placed his fingers on the keys. Sanché forced his trademark sage smile and half-turned his head to look back over his shoulder. He nodded, as though being guided by someone standing behind him, and tried to look appreciative. As he turned back, his eyes fell upon the woven basket, sitting innocuously on his nightstand, and his thoughts cut to Murielle and her small dark eyes. The smile dropped from his face. If the photograph were to be taken, it would be splashed across the front page of the newspaper and plastered to the window of every shopfront in the country. Without a doubt, Murielle would see it. Sanché, stooge of the administration.

His speculation was interrupted by the approaching sound of footfalls and excited voices in the corridor. He stood up from the desk and rushed over to the nightstand. Sanché took the basket into his hands and shook it violently, then held it up to his ear and listened to the scuttling. The voices grew louder as the procession arrived at the far side of his door and the rasping of claws against the dried grass of the basket melted into the sound of locks being opened. Sanché lay back on the bed, placed the basket on his chest, and removed the lid. As the door swung open, he stuck his hand inside and prayed for the bliss of a thousand stings.

Soundtracker

WRITING THE AD WAS a struggle. It wasn't until I was sitting at the computer—the "creative services offered" section of Craigslist open in front of me—that I realized I wasn't totally clear myself on what I was offering, let alone how to describe it to strangers. I fussed over the wording for almost an hour. *Musical Orchestrator? Audio Companion?* I finally settled on:

> *Soundtracker for hire. Multi-instrumentalist available to provide original musical accompaniment for special occasions or just hanging out at home. Make your wildest (musical) dreams come true. Competitive rates. Call anytime.*

I hit "Submit," then curled up in bed and waited for my life to begin again. Fifteen minutes later, my email chimed.

WALTER ASKED THAT WE meet at a coffee shop a few blocks from my apartment. I knew who he was before I even went inside. Through the window, I could see a lanky guy in his early thirties hunched over a table, scribbling in a spiral notebook. We shook, his hand warm and dry, mine a little damp.

"So," I said, "let me tell you a little about the service I'm, uh, prepared to offer. No, wait. I'll start again. Have you ever seen a movie? What I mean is, have you ever seen the movie *Star Wars*? Now, imagine how lifeless that film would be without John Williams's stunning arrangements. Luke Skywalker's transformation fro—"

Walter held up his palm. "What I want, what I *need*, is for someone—you—to score my life for an undetermined length of time. Can you do that?" He stared at me until I nodded.

"Good." Walter tore the page he'd been writing on out of his notebook and slid it across the table. "Here's a partial list of music I like. For inspiration."

"Oh, well, in case it wasn't clear from my ad, I'd mostly be performing my own music. I mean, I don't have the rights to anyone else's songs or anything, so if you want, like, Kanye or something, then—"

"No one's going to get litigious on you, Nathan. We're just two friends enjoying some songs and each other's company, right?"

I felt like I couldn't stop blinking. "Right. You're right."

Walter had thick hair the colour of wet hay. His nose was sharp and a little bent.

"We'll start at 10 tomorrow." He wrote his address on the corner of a fresh page, ripped it out, and handed it to me.

"We should probably discuss my fee," I said. "Because this is a pilot project, I'm offering you a reduced rate. It'll be on an hourly basis." I hadn't really thought about how the money would work. "Time-and-a-half on weekends?"

"Neither of us has done this before, have we, Nathan?" Both of us slowly shook our heads. Walter smiled without showing his teeth. "Besides, whatever, the money doesn't matter."

"But won't that screw you at tax ti—"

"Nathan. You will get paid."

"Oh. Okay, great." I wiped my hands on my jeans.

"I'll see you in the morning, then." Walter bent over his notebook and started writing, his hand cupped to block my view. I nodded and walked out to the street. The meeting took five minutes, and I never even got coffee. On the way home, I stopped at the Starbucks where I used to work, but no one I knew was on shift and I was a dollar short.

THAT NIGHT I SPENT hours poring over Walter's list — Lee Hazlewood, Kool Keith, Bauhaus, Grimes, Ennio Morricone, some disco and house music, piles of German stuff I'd never even heard of, classical, Britpop, hardcore. It hadn't occurred to me that my client might know more about music than me, and I was embarrassed to have to rip most of it off the internet. Walter couldn't have been more than five or six years older, but I already felt like his dim nephew. I listened to track after track after track until my headphones began to pinch.

The next morning, I packed my portable mixer, keyboard, battery pack, speakers, rhythm instruments, and accordion onto a handcart and pushed it fifteen blocks in the drizzle to the address Walter had given me.

Goldenview Mansion. I found his name on the intercom menu and buzzed up. The door hummed and clicked open, letting me into a lobby of thick carpet and patterned wallpaper. One of those glorious old buildings with transoms and crown moulding where nothing ever works properly. The elevator creaked like arthritis.

Walter wore the same clothes he'd worn the day before — cargo pants, black hoodie, white T-shirt — and ushered me in with the same wiry intensity.

The living room was a shrine to dead media — records, CDs, books, VHS tapes stacked everywhere — but otherwise nothing special. Ikea coffee table, saggy couch, Dali prints, a pair of lamps, one potted fern near the window. We sat down at a two-seat table in the kitchenette.

I spoke first: "So, how do you want to start this?"

Walter gestured towards the sink. "Dishes." A big, loose pile on the countertop.

"Right, so what sort of mood are you looking for?"

"You tell me."

I got up and walked to the sink. There was a window above it that looked out over a dead box-garden on the roof of the building next door. "Well, washing dishes is monotonous and you have a lot of them. The weather's pretty crap today. Something mechanical, maybe a little melancholy?"

Walter shrugged. I dug out my mini keyboard sequencer and placed it on the table. Walter got up and went to the sink. He stared out the window.

I started with a motorik 4/4 beat—*dum-dum-dum-tsh, dum-dum-dum-tsh*—then played a minor harmonic scale and looped it over the top. Walter squirted dish soap into the sink and turned on the tap. I added a sample of a woman singing "Some traditions cannot be overcome" and slowed it down to a drawl. Walter dumped the plates in the sink and began wiping. I threw in a plaintive bird cry on the sixth beat. Walter did the bowls and cups. I pulled the snare back and pushed up the hi-hat. Walter scrubbed the cutlery, adding a metallic jangle. As Walter pulled the plug and shut off the tap, I killed the beat and the spoken sample, leaving only the scale and bird cry as an echo. As the drain slurped up the last of the water, I turned the machine off. Walter stood still, his back to me.

He turned. "That was perfect." He was smiling that same small, closed-mouth smile.

"What's next?"

"Wash the floors."

"Something a little heavier, maybe?"

Walter nodded.

Later that evening, on the way out the door, he pushed a wad of bills into my hand. I counted it in the elevator on the way down. A hundred and twenty dollars. The first gig I'd ever been paid for in cash instead of beer.

TIM HAD CALLED a band meeting and suggested we all go for breakfast. When I showed up at the diner, Martin and Bread were already there, too. We ordered and made small talk over our eggs for a while. When I told them I was working on an accordion part for "All Our Parents' Basements," the conversation died on the table. Tim *ahem*ed and said, "Nate, we're out of the band." Bread and Martin stared into their coffee cups. Tim said I could keep the Bureau of Oak moniker—I'd come up with it anyway—but that the three of them would be continuing under another name. The Wise Scythes. How idiotic. They wanted a more stripped-down garage sound, no need for electronics or strings or a gong.

"But what about the accordion?"

They all looked somewhere else. I got up and left. Halfway down the block, I got a text from Tim reminding me I hadn't paid for my breakfast. I went back in and dropped a pair of fives on top of my greasy plate.

"I'VE GOT SOME ERRANDS to do."

It was only day two. "I can come back tomorrow."

Walter shook his head. "No. You're coming with me."

Half an hour later, we were on the sidewalk in front of Walter's building. Walter carried nothing. I carried maracas and a tambourine in my hands and a pair of bongo drums on a strap around my neck. My miniature drum machine stretched the breast pocket of my shirt.

While we walked, I tapped the tambourine against my thigh and *shooka-shook*ed the maracas. If Walter was aware of people staring, he didn't show it. He just bobbed his head, a full stride in front of me down the sidewalk. His legs were a lot longer than mine and I had to hustle to keep up. I felt like a real asshole.

We stopped in front of the gas station convenience store on the corner. As Walter reached for the door handle, I let my arms fall loose to my sides. Walter wheeled around. "What are you doing?"

"You're going in, right? I can't play in there."

"If you're going to be my soundtracker, Nathan, then

you have to soundtrack." Walter scowled. "Do your job."

"Okay, okay." I started it back up again, turned on the little beat maker to my approximation of tropicalismo. While Walter rooted around in the cooler, the young attendant gawked at me. Over the kid's shoulder, I could see myself on the security monitor and had to look away. Walter just nodded along.

I followed Walter down the street, to the waterfront, through the park, until we finally arrived at the big grocery store — the MegaSave. The automatic doors whispered open and pulled us in.

Walter traversed the aisles, loading the cart with cans and boxes and plastic packages. I was quickly realizing how intuitive I had to be, creating sound to match Walter's mood and gait, transitioning smoothly from one to the next. I tried to match the music to the product being selected — something upbeat and jingly for breakfast cereal, languid and soothing for soup. Some customers laughed or smiled when they saw us; others seemed angry, like we'd upset their routines. Mostly, they just pretended not to see or hear us at all.

To be truthful, I was starting to get into it, being a spectacle. While we waited in line at the cashier, I straightened up to full height and threw down a little merengue. I looked around to see who was watching, and that's when I saw Cara. She came up right behind me in line.

"What's going on, Nate?" She was holding a box of those gluten-free crackers she likes and had her hair cut into bangs. "Is everything okay with you?"

"Can't really talk right now." I leaned in so Walter couldn't hear. "I'm on the clock." I tapped the bongos louder and faster and swung my head.

Cara took a step back. "Do your parents know about this?" Her brow was so furrowed it looked like her eyebrows were trying to kiss each other. She reached out her hand and touched my elbow. "I heard about the band, you know." Past her, I could see a security guard moving towards us.

I looked back as Walter accepted his change from the cashier and began to head for the exit. I pulled my arm away and started to follow, speaking up over my own noise: "This isn't busking, if that's what you think." Before the automatic doors whooshed closed behind me, I heard Cara call my name and say else something I couldn't hear. I didn't let myself go back to check.

Outside, Walter asked who the girl was.

"No one special."

CARA HAD LIKED THAT I was in a band. We'd met at Bureau of Oak's first show, where she stood at the edge of the low stage through our whole set. While the next band was doing their soundcheck, she asked if she could buy me a drink. On our tour of the Pacific Northwest, she called me every day and would talk in a low purr about what she was doing with her free hand.

When we were serious, she said, "You should probably get a job. That student loan's not going to pay itself."

When things got bad, she said, "You're not a professional musician, Nathan. You don't even know how to play the guitar."

"BRING YOUR VIOLIN," WALTER said over the phone. "We're going to visit my niece." I suggested the accordion, but he nixed it and hung up. It was day five.

He picked me up in a cab and got me to sit up front with the driver while he stared out the window. We pulled up in front of a nondescript bungalow in the suburbs, its yard dotted with mud-spattered summer toys. Walter knocked, and an angular woman came to the door. His sister. "What the fuck, Walt?" she hissed. She glared at me over his shoulder.

"Good to see you also, Judy. This is my associate, Nathan." He nodded to me. "Is Kaylie home?"

"You can't just disappear and reappear whenever. What even goes on in your head, Walt? Do you have any fucking idea?"

"Yes, I'm sure everyone is real torn up. So, Kaylie?" The

two of them stared at each other in silence for almost a full minute.

Finally, the sister shook her head and said, "That's so fucking typical." She stomped into the house. "Kaylie! You have visitors." We followed her inside.

Kaylie was a quick and loud eight-year-old, lean like her mother and uncle, with so many plastic barrettes clipped into her hair that they clicked when she moved. Walter became a different person around her, asking goofy questions and intentionally forgetting the names of things. She brought out a stack of paintings on that cheap paper that comes in giant pads and walked Walter through the intricacies of each. He nodded thoughtfully and traced his fingers over the different arcs and splats of colour. I was trying to decipher the tone of the scene so I knew what to play, but Walter gave me a subtle shake of his head, his eyes flicking to Judy, who leaned in the doorway and fumed. After a while, he told Kaylie he needed to talk to her mom and that maybe she and I could discuss music while they went to the other room. He gave me a brief nod, stood up, and pulled Judy through a doorway, closing the door behind him.

Kaylie played the oboe at school. When I showed her my violin, she told me to play "The Devil Went Down to Georgia."

"I don't know how to play that one," I said. "Besides, kiddo, I think that's for fiddle."

Kaylie crossed her arms. "They're the same instrument, dummo."

Instead, I played her the string part of Britney Spears's "Toxic" and then—as Walter and Judy's muffled voices rose in the other room—bludgeoned my way through "Flight of the Bumblebee." I realized that I didn't really have any full songs, merely little fragments to support what other people were playing, but I could hear Judy sobbing in the other room and played anything I could, as loud as possible.

Kaylie tilted her little head. "Are you very good? I think maybe you're not very good."

Judy and Walter came through the doorway. Both wrung their hands—palms roving over knuckles, fingers interlacing—and Judy's cheeks were wet with tears. "Well, I guess that's it then." She shot me a look I couldn't fathom. Walter gave Kaylie a long hug, and then the two of us were in a cab again, heading home. I sat in the front seat and made small talk with the driver while Walter sat behind, his hands still climbing over each other.

As I was getting out, he said, "I tried, Nathan. You saw that I tried, right?"

"You did," I said.

"I wish you'd been in there." Walter reached forward and squeezed my shoulder. "The acoustics were incredible."

WE CONTINUED. WALTER WOULD putter around the apartment or eat or go to the store and I would accompany him. I studied the compositions of Philip Glass. He shifted the furniture around for better framing. I mastered the bass synth line from "Blue Monday" and put it to good use. I'd come to understand that, in the same way Walter's actions dictated how I played, I could change his movements with my music, make him bounce or sweep or plod. We'd reached music/motion symbiosis. Each reacted to the other.

During one epic session, I played for nearly six hours straight while Walter pulled box after box from his closet and loaded their contents into heavy-duty garbage bags. I recorded him hauling the bags down the stairs, across the alley, and into the yard of the boarded-up house you could see from his living room window and jumbled the sounds together into a kind of audio collage. As he dumped report cards, photographs, and a lone basketball trophy into the burning barrel there, I looped back the crackle of the flames and the hissing of wet leaves. By the hypnotized look in his eyes, I could tell I fucking nailed it.

As often as not, though, we would just sit and talk about music or watch movies. While we were watching *The Graduate*, he paused the video as Dustin Hoffman languished in the pool to "The Sounds of Silence" and said, "This is exactly what I've been talking about." We both nodded at the truth of it.

The days got longer. Sometimes I went home, sometimes I slept on his couch. Walter had a key cut for me. At some point each day, he would give me a handful of cash, which I'd shove in my wallet without counting until later. Up to a thousand dollars a week.

If Walter had a job or any other relationships or connections—other than his sister and niece—then I didn't know who they were. If I had any friends or family who gave a shit, then I didn't know who they were either. I didn't need Tim or Martin or Bread. I didn't want to be in their stupid band anyway. I didn't need my parents and their suggestions that it was time to "start taking life seriously" or that I enrol in an accounting class like my brother. I didn't need Cara. They could all go fuck themselves. I had a new gig that was better than anything they could offer. I had someone who shared my interests.

WALTER GAVE ME AN afternoon off but told me to come back in the evening. I didn't know what to do with myself, so just went home and worked on my hip hop beats for a while, then had a nap. When I returned later, Walter was fidgety and bouncier than usual. He excused himself to the bedroom to make a phone call. A few minutes later, he came out into the kitchenette and pulled a bottle of something amber-coloured from the cupboard. He poured two shots and slid one across the table. "I've got someone coming over," he said. "A friend." *Friend* sounded like it had quotation marks around it.

"Oh," I said. "Okay, cool. Do you want me to take off then?"

"No," he said quickly. "You need to be here." He reached for the bottle again and topped up our glasses.

The intercom buzzed. Soon, a young woman with glasses and mousy-brown hair stood in the apartment.

"Nathan, this is Chantelle. Chantelle, Nathan."

She smiled and touched my arm. "Walter's told me about you." Chantelle smelled like apple pie spice and sweat.

"Uh, thanks? Do you have a request?"

Walter and Chantelle spoke simultaneously — "Magnetic Fields" — and gave each other secret smiles. I pushed away my instruments and cued the music on my computer while Walter poured another round. We talked and drank and talked. Whenever Walter got up, Chantelle's eyes would track him around the room and her smile would come and go.

A short while later, I found myself in a buoyant haze. I shimmied in the kitchenette — our glasses in a sloppy line in front of me on the counter — and sang. Sang! The band never wanted me to sing, not even back-up. Chantelle hugged my waist and pointed to my pile of equipment in the corner. "Where's your guitar? I wanna hear some guitar."

Walter spun around and shouted, "Guitars are for wankers," and maybe it was the euphoria of sad music played loudly or maybe it was the liquor, but I felt like my heart was glowing out of my chest. Laughing, I twirled Chantelle, then broke away and jogged off down the hall for a piss.

When I returned from the bathroom, Walter and Chantelle were on the couch, her sweater on the floor and her hand slipped down the waist of Walter's pants. He was watching me intently.

"Oh, I...ah. Well, shit." I stumbled into my shoes and out the door. They called after me, but I didn't hear what.

I waited for the elevator, but by the time it dinged open, I found myself back down the hallway, standing outside Walter's door, my knuckles poised an inch from the wood. Up close, I could still hear the music inside. I must have stood there for a couple of minutes — swaying lightly side-to-side — when Chantelle appeared in the doorway, wearing a pair of men's boxer shorts and nothing else.

"He said you'd be back." She had a tattoo of a cartoon snail on one breast, its eye stalks crossed and tongue lolling out. "Walter says this scene is important." She took my hand and led me in.

While Chantelle disappeared into the bedroom, I turned off the music on my laptop and picked up the keyboard. I stepped down the hallway after her. Walter stood naked near the bed, one hand working his cock. When he saw me, he smiled wide enough to show his teeth. He hooked one long finger into Chantelle's boxers and pulled them down over her thighs.

I pushed some clothes off a chair in the corner and sat. Walter ran his thin hand down Chantelle's back and wedged it into the cleft of her ass. I programmed in the beats I'd been working on earlier — *boom-boom-bu-dat-tss-tss* — and slowed them to a trickle. Walter sat on the bed and took one of Chantelle's nipples into his mouth. I added some dub effects and strings. Chantelle knelt down between his legs. I looped in a Nina Simone sample. Chantelle gently pushed Walter on to the bed and climbed on top of him. I undid my pants and slid my hand inside. Both of them watched me.

The three of us stood. Walter and Chantelle moved to either side of me, tugged off my hoodie and T-shirt, lowered my jeans and underwear in one piece. "Wait," I said, turned up the volume on the keyboard and hit repeat.

Walter and Chantelle lay back on the bed. I fell into the empty space between them and let myself be enveloped in pale skin and musky smells and guiding hands and hair and mouths and hot breath on my neck.

IN THE MORNING, CHANTELLE was gone and Walter stood in the kitchen in a pair of saggy briefs. We sat at the table in front of cups of instant coffee.

"You can take today off, if you want," he said. "Yesterday was a long day."

I nodded. "Sure." I didn't know what to say about what had transpired. My words felt thick.

"We should definitely meet tomorrow, though. I have some ideas for the death scene."

"Okay, right. I can come—wait, what? What death scene?"

Walter took a sip, then stared across the cup. "Mine," he said.

BACK AT HOME, I tried to psych myself up to call Tim and the boys about getting the band back together. I put on Bureau of Oak's self-titled cassette and cranked it. After a few songs, I turned it down. Before the first side even ended, I shut it off. Maybe it was because I'd advanced so far since then, or maybe I'd just soured on the whole thing. Either way, the music was terrible; too much sound, a Brian Wilson–meets–My Bloody Valentine dense wall of shit. Rank fucking amateur, at best.

WITHOUT CALLING FIRST, I went back to Walter's and let myself in. I startled him as he sat on the floor, packing up all his albums and discs and videos to give to me.

"I don't want them, Walter. I swear, I'll throw it all straight in the trash." I held up Van Morrison's *Astral Weeks*. "Imagine this in the dumpster. That's what you'll be doing."

"Look, I've already said all the goodbyes I need to. I've given all my money to you, to Chantelle." He grabbed the jar of cash from the shelf and plunked it in front of me. "Here's the last of it. It's yours. I've made up my mind."

Walter stopped moving, and I stared at his face. He stared back. I kept waiting for him to crack a smile, to show his teeth, but his mouth remained a flat line.

"You're really going to do this," I said.

He nodded, turned away, and started to roam around the apartment again. "This is the final act." He carried a stack of books from the shelf to the table, then doubled back and put them in a bag. Moved the bag to a chair. Opened drawers and closed them.

I slumped down to the floor in front of the couch. My eyes followed him around the room. "But it's not a movie." I felt tears on my cheeks.

"It would be better if it was." Walter was pacing in tighter and tighter circles. He rushed back to the bookshelf and grabbed something else. He waved a piece of paper at me. "Look, I've even written up some suggestions for the denouement."

I took the list from him. "Joy Division? *Carmina Burana?*

Are you kidding me? I'm a musician, Walter. Not a fucking DJ."

Walter stopped moving. He crouched down and eased the paper out of my hand. "I'm sorry, Nathan. Of course, you are. You're a professional musician. And this is terribly maudlin, you're right." He folded the list and jammed it in his pocket. "I just get caught up in my own head, sometimes. I'm lucky to have found you."

I wiped my nose on my sleeve and looked up. Walter's face was scrunched with worry. "I was lucky to find you, too," I said, and meant it. By the window, the fern drooped, its leaves beginning to curl into little brown fists.

THE NEXT NIGHT, I sat at my computer and stared at the blinking cursor for over an hour before I addressed the email to caraheartnate@gmail.com and wrote "HELP" in the subject line:

> *No, I'm not okay. You were right about a lot of stuff. Everything I try to do, I'm in over my head. There's nothing I can handle on my own. I don't know how to handle this . . .*

I hit "Send," then curled up in bed and waited. A few minutes later, I heard my email chime, but it was only a bounceback: "This email address is no longer valid."

Seconds after, my phone rang. Walter said, "It's time."

I HEAVED THE CASE onto Walter's table and undid the snaps. I lifted the accordion out, shrugged on the shoulder straps, tightened the bass strap, and slid my hand through. It had been Grandpa's squeezebox, and no one else in the family wanted it when he died. I'd pulled it from a pile of old things my parents were going to take to the Sally Ann.

I stood on the other side of the door as Walter prepared the bathroom. The door was open a crack, and through it I could hear the rasp of a cigarette lighter and see flickers in the dark. A gentle splash. Then Walter spoke: "I'm ready. You can come in now."

I nudged the door open with my foot and stepped inside. The air was so dense with steam and incense I nearly lost my breath. I backed against the inside of the door to close it as my fingers began to move over the keys and buttons. The room was lit by candles clustered around the bathtub in which Walter lay.

Once my eyes adjusted to the dim light, I could see him watching me. I sat down on the toilet lid and played a glacial "Jesus Don't Want Me for a Sunbeam." During a drawn-out pause, I heard Walter whisper, "Like Wes Anderson. Cinematic." I compressed the bellows. I played louder.

My eyes didn't know where to go. Everything they fell on was wrong. Walter's thick hair plastered to his skull from the damp. The candlelight and incense smoke making roving ghosts against the tile. His body distorted by the water, genitals rudely breaking the surface. The glint off the straight razor resting in the soap dish. Walter's unblinking eyes. His long face, grim in its placidness.

I finished the song. Walter's hand rose from the water, towards the soap dish. I began to play a composition of my own. It was written in the sad, French style, and I'd never played it for anyone, not Cara, not the boys in the band. This was its debut.

Walter's hand faltered, then dropped back to rest empty on his thigh. He closed his eyes as I let my fingers find the keys.

You, the Truthteller

YOU WATCH MARCIA at the lecture desk haphazardly shoving papers into a manila envelope. A fellow student, the dim boy with the sharp Adam's apple and wispy moustache, stops in the doorway and says something that makes her laugh before he files out with everyone else. When Marcia laughs, she half-covers her mouth with her hands, a sure sign of poor self-esteem, and no wonder. You continue to watch as she removes the same tired apple from her bag, which she again failed to eat during break, in order to dig for her keys. Once everyone else has gone, you call out from the rear of the lecture theatre, where you sit with your feet up on the back of the seat in front of you, your rich baritone voice startling her.

She asks if she can help you with anything, Henry, and do you have any questions? You respond that yes, you have several comments, and is she interested in any feedback on today's lecture? She hesitates, and even from metres away, you can see something flash behind her eyes, panic perhaps or awe; your eyesight is keen, like an osprey, and she becomes a rainbow trout, her scales flashing in the sunlight as she desperately circles a shallow pool. Eventually, she pulls herself together and says it's important that she get feedback from students and she is always looking for ways to improve the classroom experience. She says she has noticed you've taken a keen interest and wouldn't you be more comfortable speaking to her at a closer distance? You reply that no, you are perfectly comfortable where you are due to your sharp hearing, and additionally, because of your large, masculine frame, it is obviously preferable that you be able to sprawl out over the seats rather than be hunched down in a single chair like a meek child.

You begin by asking her to present her credentials. She pauses, blushing, and claims not to have them, that she doesn't carry any sort of certification around with her, but assures you nonetheless that she has both a B.A. in film studies and an M.F.A. with a focus on film and media arts. When you ask her from where, she replies the University of Regina. You laugh and say, well, that explains a lot. She leans forward on her stool and grips the edges of the desk's lectern, defensive and insecure, and asks what do you mean by that?

You tell her she should do her research more carefully.

She asks if you could be more specific, please. You go on to explain that, for most of today's lecture, you felt confused as to whether or not you were even talking about the same film. You tell Marcia that you found yourself wondering, at various junctures, whether or not she had even seen the film in question, or if she, as you suspect, had just read some reviews and synopses online and quickly cobbled something together on the subway here.

Instantly, you can tell that you've struck a nerve. As you observe, Marcia closes her eyes for a second and takes a sharp breath. When she opens them, her mouth dips into a little half-smile and you know that she knows that you know that she is feeling terribly sheepish at being called out and exposed as a fraud, and you prepare yourself to receive the inevitable apology, the you-got-me-Henry with accompanying shrug and searching, outstretched palms.

But, surprisingly, sadly, Marcia is not yet willing to make this admission. Instead, she claims to have seen the film no less than ten times and has, in fact, had two different essays published on the topic in two different peer-reviewed journals devoted to the study of film. Also, is that sufficient, Henry?

You re-cross your muscular legs and tell her you've been observing her from your aerie at the back of the room and how it has become clear to you that all her bravado, all her authoritative lecturing, is only a smokescreen designed to distract from the fact that she knows she is out of her depth, a dilettante, a dabbler. As if to prove exactly this point, Marcia smirks and leans back in her chair, swivelling the seat slightly from side to side in an attempt, you suppose, to give the impression of a cat about to pounce. Through her unnecessary swagger and impotent smirk, Marcia says she is disappointed and concerned, Henry, that this is all you have taken away from our classroom time together.

With great patience, you explain to her that you are as adroit a judge of character as anyone who's ever lived, and that you know that she knows that, which is why she is so often dismissive of the facts you present in class. She coughs up a shrill, anxious laugh and says no, Henry, that is not why she has dismissed some of your opinions, and are you aware that there are several dozen other people in the class, all of whom have a right to speak?

Marcia is playing dirty now. You laugh again and say, who? Those people? Does she mean the inane, mustachioed boy, whose favourite film is almost certainly *The Wrath of Khan* or some other campy mess? Is she referring to the triad of Sandra Bullock fans, who giggle in the corner for two hours twice a week? Can she be suggesting that the old woman in the beret, who apparently believes that the genre started and ended with *Breakfast at Tiffany's*, is working, is thinking, on the same level? How are they supposed to be able to grasp the subtlety of Kurosawa's early work or understand the importance of space in American road cinema of the sixties? Those people, Marcia? Those people are not even of the same species. The comparison, you say, is grossly inadequate.

As you observe, she begins to nod her head slowly, mesmerized by the succinctness of your words, and says that she thinks she gets it now, Henry, and are these questions and criticisms in regards to today's returned essay? She asks if you are disappointed with the comments she's provided. You inform Marcia that you do not believe in disappointment — only consternation. You tell her it is evident that she has wholly misunderstood what you have achieved within the essay, which you accede is perhaps understandable considering the scope of your writing. Marcia clasps her hands together and rests them on the desktop and says that you do realize, Henry, don't you, that you eclipsed the required word count by several thousand words, that the assignment was to provide a concise summation not a multi-paged diatribe?

You smile, benevolently, as you grasp the full extent of her bewilderment. Those people, your classmates, have lowered the bar so severely that it has dropped below the horizon. Your essay stands in such stark contrast to those of the others that it is as though Marcia has stepped from a darkened room into the mid-day sun, the piercing rays momentarily blinding her.

You grant Marcia amnesty and tell her not to worry, you're not angry with her, everyone makes mistakes. You hold the offending essay high over your head, your biceps testing the fabric of your shirt, material straining to contain your brawn, and tell her that she will have to pay more attention during her re-read. Perhaps a thesaurus will help.

Marcia closes her eyes again, bracing herself against the desk as your words seep in. She sighs and looks up, humbled, and suggests, if you are to continue this conversation, that you come down to the front row, that her voice is strained from a day of lecturing. It is unnecessary for you to repeat yourself, so you just continue to wave the essay back and forth, in a slow, hypnotic arc, the precise movement of a condor's wing. She gazes up at you, breathing deeply for a moment, daunted and exhilarated, then stands and steps out from behind the desk, crosses the floor, and climbs the steps towards you, caught now in your magnet's pull, helpless. She sits down in a seat in the row in front of you and a little off to the side and turns to regard you, silently holding out a trembling hand, in which you place the stapled stack of papers. As you transfer the essay, your formidable finger grazes her frail hand, and she retracts it quickly, shivering with pleasure. She says that she will read it again but can't guarantee a change of grade. She asks is that everything, Henry, do you need anything else from me today?

Holding her tender heart in your powerful hand, you gently acknowledge that this all must be difficult for her to hear, that confronting oneself and one's limitations can often be a painful, harrowing experience and that, hopefully, she comprehends this is for her own good. You lightly chide her for her misinterpretations; your goal, after all, is not to humiliate but simply to guide. You know she is struggling with the truth. But, you tell her, you feel it is vital that the two of you clear the air now, that you maintain an open dialogue, for the health and wellbeing of your relationship. You tell her it would be too difficult, too complicated to have this conversation later, once things have begun to progress on a more intimate, physical level.

Marcia is floored by your generosity of spirit. You have rendered her speechless. She stares at you, mouth slightly agape, lost in the unfathomable blue of your eyes. You allow her a minute to take it all in; your aristocratic nose and robust lips, the definition of your jaw, your cascading mane of dense, tawny hair. Her thoughts become tangled. She says what relationship, Henry?

You tell her it is perfectly natural to feel confused, that it would be challenging, even for someone as highly evolved as yourself, to have to suppress so many feelings. You explain to her that for weeks she has been a simmering pot, just a mere degree from boiling over, but you are pleased she has been able to control herself and still maintain a modicum of professionalism. You understand the stress she has been under, the strength of her emotions disrupting her ability to teach, hence the shoddy lectures, the subpar interpretation of your essay. You tell her you can't imagine the torture she's been through, keeping her passion hidden while the prying eyes of the troglodytes around you wait for a slip-up so they can go running to the dean. It must be so difficult for the rest of them, you say, to witness such an intense rapport, the air around them crackling with kinetic energy, their jealousy dissolving into bitterness.

Marcia's never felt this way before. She says she doesn't know what to say, Henry. She casts her eyes down and swallows hard, thinking, no doubt, about your weight pressing down against her. She shudders, with anticipation, and pulls her blazer tighter around her, covering herself with her arms, to prevent her pale skin from breaking into goosebumps.

You tell Marcia that you imagine it presumably will take some time for her nervousness around you to subside but that, over time, you will begin to appear less intimidating and the two of you will become equals, in a way. That being said, you do have some expectations that will need to be addressed. Obviously, due to the archaic rules regarding student/teacher fraternization, she will have to resign from her post. You joke about how that shouldn't be too difficult for her, as this job is clearly such a poor fit anyway. Now that she has captured your attention, she will want to work hard to maintain it, and you suggest that she study Isabella Rossellini in David Lynch's 1986 film *Blue Velvet* for pointers. You recommend that she seek out a good diction coach.

Marcia stands and locks her watery eyes to yours. She says, is this a weird joke, Henry? She is so overcome, you're a bit embarrassed for her. This is no joke, you say. Her mission, to pique your interest, to alert you to her intentions, has been successful, and over time, you will likely come to feel as strongly about her as she clearly does about you. Though she will unquestionably miss these times together, these Tuesdays and Thursdays from 6 p.m. until 8 p.m., she will come to see their absence as an unavoidable aspect of relationship building; a necessary, if minor, sacrifice.

You reach out your hand to push a lock of mousy hair from her face, but she denies her excitement, pulls away, not yet ready to succumb to her desires. As you watch, Marcia, weakened and ashen from the dizzying freedom now whirling around inside her, stands and rushes down the steps towards her desk. She sweeps her papers and envelopes into her arms, carelessly knocking the tired apple to the floor, and disappears through the door, too affected to look back.

You stand now and stretch, your giant's bulk shrinking the room, your fingertips brushing the ceiling and walls. You walk down the steps, your virility challenging the very integrity of the building, floorboards whining and groaning beneath you as they acknowledge your strength. At the desk you stop, letting one massive foot hover over the fallen apple before crushing it with the satisfying crunch of a foe's skull. You turn and gaze across the room, benign seats cowering together for protection, and shout, your voice laying waste to all that lies before you.

You are loved, you bellow. You are loved. You are loved. You are loved.

Aunts and Uncles

THE NEWS OF MY aunt and uncle's divorce hardly came as a surprise. I'd run into my uncle once downtown and had been too quick to admit I was doing nothing, so he'd shepherded me onto the patio of a chain restaurant for a cheap pint. "Girls like *that*." He nodded across the street. "You could do all sorts of things with them, I bet." And girls they were—not young women, but actual children—clustered, giggling, taking photos with their phones. Uncle Glen was my aunt's second husband, and this was the only time I'd been with him one-on-one, but I knew right there what his deal was. He winked, and I felt kind of sick.

Aunt Cindy was a mess, for real. One minute she'd be sobbing, leaving snot and bronzer smears on the shoulder of my only decent shirt, and the next lambasting me for still living at home. She kept telling me to go outside, leaving the front door open, like I was a starling who'd flown in by mistake and was knocking myself senseless trying to get out. I knew she wanted to get off Mom's loveseat and claim my room, so I let it slide. She asked me once if I could get her some ecstasy, but I pretended like I didn't understand what she meant.

MOM MOSTLY WORKED GRAVEYARD, so Aunt Cindy got the car during the day. When I asked her to drive me to the good pet store to get filter pads for my aquarium, she made a big stink out of how she wasn't a goddamn chauffeur and could I get her another blanket but then a few seconds later bounced right up off the couch in the middle of Judge Judy's final decision and said fine.

In the car, she seemed agitated and kept flipping the radio between the country station and TalkTalk: All Talk Radio. When I told her to take a right on Kenickie, she just barrelled straight through the intersection.

"You missed it," I said.

Instead of answering, she shouted the chorus of Aerosmith's "I Don't Want to Miss a Thing" a few times, then rolled down all the windows at once, so the wind was too loud to talk. She kept driving, through the Big Box district and into a dodgy suburb, before taking a hard left and thundering down an alley behind a street with no trees. She pulled over next to a splintered fence with the gate hanging open and yanked the keys out.

"We're here," she said. She got out and went through the gate. I sat for a minute then went in after her.

We stood in the backyard of the junky little bungalow she'd briefly shared with Uncle Glen. I recognized it from once before — a few years earlier when the two of them had their wedding reception there and everyone said later how Glen could have at least cleaned up all the cigarette butts first.

Aunt Cindy walked up the three steps to the back door, jammed a key in and fiddled around. It wouldn't open. She told me to check the windows, but they all had those metal security grids over them. She threw her shoulder into the door. She was crying again.

"I don't think that's a very great idea," I said.

"Well, you're not a very great nephew." She slammed into the door again, then turned back to me. "If you don't help me, Carter, you're basically helping him."

I nervously checked the houses on either side and down the alley, but the whole neighbourhood was more-or-less abandoned. I kicked at the door a couple of times, but it didn't budge.

Aunt Cindy looked wildly around the yard before rushing over to a big concrete birdbath on a wide pedestal in the corner near the fence. "Glen loves to watch the little birds while he smokes," she said. "You don't know what I've seen." Crouching, with her hair plastered down in some spots and sticking out in others, she looked like she was going to crack, so I went over to help her tip it. We shoved and rocked the birdbath, but it must have been cemented into the earth and didn't give any more than the door.

ON THE WAY TO the pet store, we didn't talk. Our sleeves were damp from the bird water. She left one of the windows partially down so the car was pulsing with that *thwub-thwub-thwub* sound that makes your brain hurt. Once we stopped, she came inside with me like we were on a normal family outing.

While I was in the fish aisle, Aunt Cindy talked to a man near the counter. Her hair had calmed down, and she'd pushed up her wet sleeves. She laughed loud, then touched his elbow and referred to me as her younger brother. He was buying the same brand of filter pads as me, and we talked about tetras and cichlids for a minute until she pinched the back of my arm and I went over to pretend to look at the plastic castles. She wrote her number on the back of his receipt. After the man left, Aunt Cindy didn't want to wait anymore and went to the car while I paid.

When I opened the car door, she was gripping the dashboard in both hands, like she wanted to break a chunk off.

Across the street, the man from the pet store stood at the bus stop, near a group of children silently texting in their private school kilts. The man looked over to us and waved, the bag of filter pads bobbing against his thigh.

"Look at them," Aunt Cindy spat. "Girls like that."

A FEW DAYS LATER, I woke to my aunt flicking my aquarium light on and off. The betta fish was swimming all around like it was hammered.

"Fish don't like that," I said. "What time is it?"

"What time are *you*?" Aunt Cindy said. She turned on the overhead light and tugged hard at the duvet. "Get up, let's go." She was wearing a John Deere ball cap and looked like she hadn't slept much.

"Stop that. Go where?" I wrapped my legs around the covers and shielded my groin.

She stopped tugging and smiled down at me. "Just errands. Nothing weird, I swear."

"Hmm." The way she said it, I didn't really believe her. I could hear Mom snoring in the other bedroom.

"I'll buy you a breakfast burrito." She sort of sang the words.

I must have looked skeptical because she started chanting, "Buree-TOH, buree-TOH, buree-TOH." She sat on the end of the bed and patted my feet in time to the chant.

AFTER THE DRIVE-THRU, we drove out to the employment office so Aunt Cindy could get some forms, then on to the drugstore for cotton balls and nicotine gum. I didn't see why she needed my help, but she played the radio at a reasonable volume and asked me regular questions, like whether I wanted to go back to school or was I still happy selling calendars.

"It's the best kiosk in the mall," I said. "I'm learning things I'll never learn in college."

"Yeah, probably." Aunt Cindy veered across two lanes and pulled over at the side of the road. She rifled through her purse until she found a CD, which she slid into the player. "Just one more quick stop, then we're good." She notched up the volume and the opening chords of Heart's "Barracuda" rumbled out. She merged back into traffic and started singing the guitar parts: *Dun-diddlun-diddlun-diddlun—*"

"Can you drop me at home?" It felt like the car was filled with too many galloping horses.

"—*diddlun-dun-dun-dun...mwow!*" Aunt Cindy tapped her thumbs against the steering wheel. "You already ate the burrito, Carter. You signed the contract."

She picked up speed and plowed through a yellow, almost hitting some high-school girls at the crosswalk, then back into the same neighbourhood as earlier in the week. She slowed going past Glen's house but didn't stop. Just as the song ended, she pulled up in front of a three-storey apartment building. One of the front apartments had a shower curtain instead of drapes and there was another bird bath on the lawn, but it was dry. Aunt Cindy got out and came around to open my door.

She ran her fingernail down the columns of names on the apartment intercom before she stopped at one. It read *R. Colbert*. She turned to me and said, "She's not going to let me in, so you do the talking," then mashed down all the buttons except R. Colbert's with her palms.

"Wait, what am I supposed to —"

"Hello?" came an elderly voice.

Aunt Cindy silently jabbed her finger at me then at the console and made like she was going to boot my shin.

"Hydro," I shouted. "We're the Hydro attendant. Hydro."

The door clicked open.

WE STOOD OUTSIDE R. Colbert's door. I asked Aunt Cindy, "Who is this person?"

"I did some sleuthing. Glen was sticking it to her the same time he was sticking it to me."

I shook my head because I didn't want to think about Uncle Glen sticking anything to anyone or my aunt having anything stuck to her.

"Anyway," Aunt Cindy continued, "she's blocked my number, so this is the only way. I need to talk to her." She pushed me closer to the door and hunched down behind my back. "You knock."

I gave three soft taps against the door and three harder ones when nothing happened. I did it some more, but no one came. We put our ears to the door. Silence.

Aunt Cindy knelt down and propped open the mail slot. She took off her hat and tried to look inside, then stuck her mouth to it and stage-whispered, "Rhonda, are you there? I know about the sex with Glen and it doesn't matter. But do you know about the bad things, too?" After a minute, she dropped the flap and let her forehead rest against the wood. Her shoulders were shaking.

I stood there until she was ready to get up.

AUNT CINDY DRANK THREE glasses of red before I finished my beer. Her hair was all mashed down and there were sweat rings under her arms. She swung her head looking around the bar and seemed to notice me again for the first time. "What secrets are you keeping, Carter? I can't invest any more in you until I know." She leaned her head forward so her chin was resting inside her wineglass. "Every minute is an investment I might not get back."

A few things swirled through my brain, but I didn't think they were the kind of secrets she was talking about, so I shook my head. "You're invested in me?"

"I'm not sure." Aunt Cindy sighed and leaned back in her chair. "You don't ever know anyone, not ever. Fish guy still hasn't called." She pulled a few bills out of her purse and dropped them on the table, then spread her arms out. "This is it, Carter, this is all there is to love." She slumped forward and downed the last few drops of wine, then pushed the table away from her so it hit me in the ribs.

As she stood and swayed and then lurched away, I remembered how Aunt Cindy had tried to teach me to slow dance before Junior High Prom. She'd cued up "Love Hurts" and put her hands on my shoulders. While we shuffled back and forth, she said I should maintain regular eye contact and, if no teachers were watching, how I could pull the girl I was dancing with closer and seamlessly slide my hands from her waist to her bum. Mom would never have told me that. The song seemed to go on for hours.

OUTSIDE, THE SUN WAS low in the sky, so everything was glowing with that perfect orange light. I found my aunt trying to line up the key with the car's lock. She teetered into the door, then righted herself.

I stepped towards her. "I don't think that's a good idea."

Aunt Cindy squinted at me, mascara framing her cheekbones. "You're a good boy." She wiggled the key onto the lock and turned.

I reached over to take her keys from her, but she batted my hand away. "I'm tired," she said. I grabbed at her wrist and she gave me a good kick, right in the ankle bone. I went behind her and hugged and lifted her until she dropped the keys. I was surprised how light and fragile she felt. Once she dropped them, I picked the keys up and hucked them as far as I could.

It was a beautiful throw, a high arc that made the keys flash in the last of the light. It was like they kept going up and up, and they never wavered, and they never fell.

You Better Run

I'VE NEVER BEEN THE jealous type. If Julie sits on Kenny's lap or grinds up against another girl at the Carleton Arms when "Hit Me with Your Best Shot" comes on, I just laugh along because I'm part of the fun. I know when she does things like that it's not because I'm lacking something but because the other person has something that Julie needs. If she needs to run her hands through Kenny's beard, who am I to tell her she can't? If I was ever interested in someone else, I wouldn't want her to put limitations on me either, probably. Still, I was a little disappointed to find the shoes.

I'd come home from work on my lunchbreak because Skyler, my boss at eXtreme LaserTag Plus, said I looked like a dumbshit possum and needed to shave. Even though Skyler's so young, he has very professional expectations when it comes to a work environment. I know when he gives me a hard time it's because he only wants what's best for the company and — by association — what's best for me.

When I let myself into the apartment, I could hear Julie doing yoga or something in the bedroom, so I let her be and went to the bathroom. I lathered up and shaved my neck and jaw and the little moustache I was starting. I tried to be careful, but when I was done I saw that blood and shaving cream got all over my uniform collar, so I had to interrupt Julie anyway to get my clean one. The bedroom door was locked. I heard Julie quietly say "F**k" and then yell, "I've got my period." I've always tried to be respectful of female things, so I waited outside the door until she was ready.

When she opened up, Julie was wearing my housecoat. Wind was blowing the curtains around until she went and shut the window. I told her I needed my other uniform shirt. Julie said I should have called first and that she would have ironed and delivered it for me. I was telling her about how it was because of the moustache, not the shirt, that I was home, and that's when I saw the shoes under the bed. They were Reeboks. I asked her where they'd come from.

"They're probably yours," she said. "You look really sexy in that shirt. I'm getting in the shower." She pulled the robe tight and left the room. I heard the lock on the bathroom door click.

The shoes weren't mine. The laces were all knotted up, and the insides were dark and vinegary. They were size 11s, like an athlete might wear. I usually wear an 8½, so I had to pull my winter socks over my regular socks for them to fit. I reminded myself about how Julie taught me that being jealous is like making yourself drink a mayonnaise jar full of poison.

Back at work, Skyler said the shoes made me look like a dumbshit kangaroo, but they didn't violate the dress code so I could keep them on. I thanked him and went back behind the concession counter, where no one can see my feet anyway. While I waited for the latest round of taggers to finish, I crouched down and ate a pack of licorice because I didn't get lunch. I was glad Skyler didn't see me. Even though I paid for the Twizzlers, he still would've considered it time theft.

Julie was out when I got home. I heated up some casserole and watched *Jeopardy*. I kept the sneakers on and let myself put my feet up on the coffee table, even though I'm not supposed to do that. During the commercials, I closed my eyes and tried to will my feet to expand to fill the shoes, but nothing happened. When I heard Julie come in, I put my feet back on the floor. She went into the bathroom without saying anything. I didn't ask where she'd been, but I wanted to.

I kept wearing the shoes all week, even though they gave me a fungus like athletes might get. I liked the way they looked, and my whole body got so warm because of all the socks. Maybe even Skyler thought they looked good because he didn't call me a dumbshit anything all week. I wore them inside the apartment, which wasn't allowed, but if Julie noticed, she didn't say.

On Friday night, we met after work at the Carleton like usual. Julie and I sat with Kenny and everyone and drank Coors. I thought maybe someone would say how the Reeboks made me seem taller, but no one did. I gave Julie some quarters I'd been saving so she could load the jukebox. When "Love Is a Battlefield" came on, she pulled Kenny over by his beard and whipped her hair around. I smiled like always and watched for a minute, but then all of a sudden I was right between them on the dance floor. I nudged Kenny back with a steady hand and he slunk back to his beer. It was like I was being guided. Julie looked so surprised.

I don't usually like to dance because everyone says I have no rhythm, but Julie stayed tight with me on the floor, all the way through "We Belong" and "Heartbreaker." She rubbed her breasts against my chest and I felt blood rush to my penis, so I had to kind of crouch over while I was dancing so no one would see.

Back at home, Julie started pulling her clothes off, right there in the living room. She led me over to the couch and tugged open the snaps of my uniform shirt. I bent down to slip off the Reeboks so I could get out of my pants, but

Julie pushed my hand between her legs and said, "Leave the shoes on." As she pulled me into her, I wished whoever originally owned the shoes could see me and how I might be an athlete, same as him. Julie shouted, "Harder," and her nails dug deeper into my skin, and I wondered if anyone had ever explained to him about how jealousy is a dangerous sword.

The Passion and the Fugue
of Edward Frank:
A Profile by Jane Gopnik

E DWARD "WEEDIE" FRANK IS a challenging man to track down; he is nothing short of elusive in describing the location of his new apartment. And while the door buzzer identifies his unit as "Occupied," the space itself is hardly that; it's as spartan and deliberate as the plates he delivers as sous-chef for Yaletown bistro HuitNeufHuit. Sparseness aside, there is something disjointed about the apartment. Though the front hall is neatly lined with recently emptied moving boxes, many of the apartment's items are freshly purchased—the burgundy towels hung perfectly on the bathroom rod, the gleaming stainless steel toaster on the kitchen countertop, and the opened box of condoms buried in his underwear drawer. The result is a dizzying combination of foreign and familiar. When asked why he was so quick to replace his old, reliable toaster with this new, sleek model, Frank replies, "Jane!? What the hell are you doing here? How did you even — Jesus Christ, is that broken glass? Did you climb the fire escape?"

The fieriness of these queries succinctly captures both Frank's questioning nature and the depth of his passion. It's these traits that have allowed him to climb many rungs of Vancouver's culinary ladder in a relatively short time. After fruitlessly toiling in retail and fast food jobs for nearly a decade, Frank returned to school in the late 2000s, attending the city's prestigious International Cooking Institute. After *stages* at Spanish eatery Viva! and much-lauded local landmark Cucina Genoa, Frank joined the HuitNeufHuit team as a line cook in 2011. He fervidly believes in continuously asking himself what he can do to advance his cooking; it is this intensity and drive that gained him the title of sous in his first nine months, a position he's held ever since. The restaurant management speak highly of Frank and consider him an integral part of the team, with front-of-house manager Timothy Lee stating, "Like I told you before, miss, this area is for staff only. If I see you here again, I'm calling the police." With such words, one gets the feeling that Frank's star has only begun to rise.

As talented as he is though, Frank quickly acknowledges

that he couldn't have done it alone: "I worked under some great chefs at the Institute and my parents have been very supportive." With some urging, he continues, "Yes, there were other people in my life at the time who were supportive, too, I guess. Is that what you wanted to hear, Jane?"

Despite the parental encouragement he claims to have received, life on the home front was not always so easy for Frank. His father's career as a tile salesman meant that the family was always on the move, living in almost four different houses across the Lower Mainland in his first eighteen years alone. This near-constant movement created in Frank a feeling of rootlessness, making it difficult for him to maintain serious relationships for much longer than a year and three months. Of his childhood, Frank says, "I had food and shelter and loving, active parents. It was great—a really stable environment. Not that you would know anything about that." What wasn't so great was his parents' divorce in 2003, a situation which left Frank emotionally wounded and deeply commitment-phobic.

While his father, John, refuses to comment, Frank's mother, Marilyn, agrees to a telephone interview after several requests. A stern, disapproving woman, perpetually locked in a state of silent judgment, Marilyn says, "Edward was just the sweetest boy and, as you know, very intelligent and sensitive to the needs of others. When his father and I divorced, Edward was terrific about the whole thing. I've never held any ill will towards my ex-husband at all, and the three of us still get together for dinner regularly. My son understood that, for a relationship to really work, it has to be equally satisfying to both partners and that if one person is unhappy, then both are unhappy." Before hanging up the phone and returning to her life of never really giving people a chance, Marilyn adds, "Do you get what I'm saying here, Jane? Sometimes things just run their course. I hope you can grow to accept that, and soon. I mean, it was nice getting to know you for a bit and everything, but please don't call here again."

Frank is reticent to discuss the specifics of the relationship his mother alludes to, but on good authority, it was an intense connection with a dynamic young woman, a coupling notable for both its voracious desire and deep, mutual respect, which came to an unceremonious halt two months ago, when Frank announced that he needed a "break," whatever the fuck that means. Though Frank's closest friends appear confident that he will be able to survive this temporary parting, they too find his choice to suddenly move out on a Tuesday afternoon, while his dedicated girlfriend was taking a scrapbooking class at Michaels, inexplicable. When asked repeatedly what caused the rift, long-time friend Mike Grisham seems mystified and finally asks, "Gee, I wonder?"

One likely reason behind the trial separation lies in

Frank's immersion in Vancouver's restaurant and nightlife culture. Like many young chefs, he has dabbled in the drugs and alcohol that fuel the industry. "Oh my God. I smoked pot like three times and, as I told you, it just made me sleepy," he says. "Please stop calling me 'Weedie.'" Under these tumultuous circumstances, Frank has made some decisions he must certainly regret; sadly, it is improbable that, without the tender care and loving support that a dependable life-partner can provide, he will be able to beat this crushing addiction.

The culmination of all these emotional elements — a nomadic childhood and splintered home life, the stress of the professional kitchen and seductive pull of intoxicants, the paralyzing fear of a relationship that seems too good to be true — is Frank's increasing secrecy. It takes hours of digging through jacket pockets, poring over waste bin contents, and taping together shredded paperwork to begin to answer some of the questions that Frank won't. However, even these expired bus transfers, receipts for sesame bagels, and tickets for matinee showings of *The Hobbit: The Desolation of Smaug* provide little information about how he spends his time now. More telling are mementos like the one nestled between his bed's immaculate pillows — a miniature sock monkey. It's a gift, no doubt, from one of the female foodies that troll the city's vibrant restaurant scene looking for fresh meat, probably Vanessa. When

asked about the origin of the stuffed toy, Frank is predict-
ably evasive: "This is fucked, Jane. You're paying for that
window."

Here, Frank inevitably stumbles across the rawest of
truths: he *can't* continue like this. Until Weedie wakes from
this dissociative state — this emotional paralysis — we shall
all, in one way or another, be paying for that window.

The Murderess and The Heap

I'D BEEN SENT BY my firm to a conference in Calgary for the week, and on my final night, Paddy threw a party at his condo in my honour. My brother's friends were intimidating, loud and sharp in their criticism of the government. The space was spare and aggressively modern, walls hung with concert posters for bands I'd never heard of. I understood from the conversation that we were eating Korean food.

As I pushed pickled vegetables around my plate, I overheard Paddy telling some friends that our parents were dead, swallowed by an avalanche while snowshoeing in Lake Louise. In gruesome detail, he described their claustrophobic final minutes, as they gasped for breath in the freezing dark. I wasn't sure what Mother and Father would find more egregious—the lie or the suggestion that they were the type of people who enjoyed the outdoors. At the first opportunity, I pulled Paddy into the kitchen.

"Why would you even say that?"

"Well, they may as well be dead, those fucking gargoyles," Paddy had slurred and laughed and laughed until he nearly choked. "I'm sorry, Mitch, that was harsh. There have never been two people more deserving of each other." He raised his glass. "Long live The Murderess and The Heap."

I STEERED MY NISSAN up the wide curve of my parents' driveway, tires bumping over the dull, red bricks. Their house stood monstrous against a backdrop of pines, portly white rhododendrons spaced between the first-floor windows. I turned off the motor and counted backwards from two hundred, visualizing each number as I spoke. Black numerals against a white background in a sans serif font.

Mother greeted me at the door, glass of shiraz cupped snugly in one manicured hand, auburn hair piled hat-like on top of her head, trademark pearls winking in the sunlight. Heels, skirt, makeup—flawless. Despite leaving Portsmouth nearly forty years before, a vestige of England still remained in her voice. Consciously held, I suspected.

"Hello, Mitchell dear. Good to see you." She leaned forward, proffering a pale cheek to kiss. I complied. "Shoes, please." I slipped my loafers onto the small mat near the door and herded them into a neat pair with my foot.

At Mother's direction, I emptied a mahogany credenza of its burden of Royal Wedding plates and ceramic mallards before manhandling it across the living room floor. As I worked, Mother leaned against a side table and sipped her wine, occasionally smoothing an invisible wrinkle out of her skirt without putting her glass down.

I was never sure of what Mother did with her time. Though I'd witnessed her in the back garden wearing her broad-brimmed yellow sun hat, spade and chardonnay in hand, I'd never seen her dig or even crouch. I knew my parents employed an elderly landscaper to do the real work. Mother was similarly adept at pulling a finished roast from the oven without ever seeming to prep or wash a dish. I had never seen her sweat.

As I finished shuffling the credenza into its new home along the opposite wall, Mother said, "Thank you, dear. I would have asked your father to do it, but he's at work again. On a Sunday, if you can imagine. You'll stay for dinner, I hope?" A command dressed as an invitation.

I nodded.

"Make yourself comfortable in the television room." She clicked off towards the kitchen.

The TV room was one of the few areas of the house under Father's jurisdiction. Its walls held many paintings of boats. One end of the couch was heavily indented, cushions concave. I sat at the other end, staring at the enormous black screen. Several dusty trophies crowned the television. Like his thick neck and blockish frame, they were holdovers from his early days as a rugby champ. Father had quit the sporting life before I was born to concentrate instead on his career as a tax lawyer. He did not discuss his work, other than in the most peremptory way, and I was discouraged from asking, despite our mutual love of numbers. When not at the office, Father spent his time at the Oak Bay Yacht Club, sitting at the bar with other greying, slab-like men in jackets with gold crests.

At the sound of jingling keys, I sprung up and returned to the foyer. Father stood just inside the door, tan overcoat over navy jacket over white shirt with navy tie. In one hand, he held two leather briefcases; in the other, an umbrella, hat, and keys. He was attempting to pry one shoe off with the other without bending or releasing anything, his breathing strained and audible. "Goddamned shit," he muttered. "Fucking goddamn."

"Hello, Father. Can I give you a hand?"

He looked up and grunted, kicking off one shoe in the direction of the mat. He held up his other foot and wiggled it impatiently. I'd have preferred to help with the bags, but Father wasn't a young man anymore. I knelt and undid the laces and removed the shoe. Still in his coat, Father turned and thumped up the stairs to his second-floor office. As I organized his shoes next to mine, his door slammed shut.

A FEMALE FRIEND OF Paddy's, a redhead who wore sunglasses inside, had come over to where I was sitting alone. She squatted in front of me and put her hand on my knee.

"I'm so sorry for your loss," she said. Reluctant to expose my brother as a liar, I thanked her for her concern.

"I'm sure they were good people."

"Oh." I was barely able to make out her eyes behind the dark glass. "They were very complicated, but yes, lovely people." I wished Paddy hadn't put me in this position. I've never had the stomach for fibs.

She dropped her hand away and dragged a chair up beside me. "So, what do you do?"

"I'm an accountant."

She pulled a face. "No, I know that. I mean, what do you do outside of work?" I could still feel where her hand had been.

"Nothing," I'd said. "Really, nothing."

The woman laughed. "So, what, you just lie fetal in the dark, waiting for death to come?"

Around me, the music and talking seemed to get louder, but the woman didn't notice and continued to smile.

"I'm sorry, I need to go to the bathroom." I stood and

quickly left the room. I closed the bathroom door and sat on the toilet lid; if I waited long enough, she would move on to another conversation. I rarely spoke to people my own age, let alone women. Their interests always baffled me, and I had so little to say.

DURING DINNER, MOTHER MADE a number of queries about my job; about friends I hadn't seen since high school; about whether or not I was dating anyone. I answered vaguely but optimistically—a technique I'd been cultivating to help maintain a light and pleasant atmosphere. When I had told Dr. Matthews about this method, he suggested it wasn't the healthiest choice. While I was prone to agree with him, I found that specific answers were far too easy to critique.

"Have you spoken to your brother lately?"

I thought of Paddy's description of Mother's mangled body being airlifted off the mountain, how difficult it was for the search-and-rescue team to harness her because she was frozen at such an unlikely angle. To avoid lying, I half-shrugged—another tactic I sometimes employed.

"Oh, that's a shame. It would be lovely to see Patrick, it's been ages," she said. "It's too bad Calgary is so gauche, what with all that new money."

I nodded in solidarity. "Too true." I placed another forkful of beef in my mouth and chewed slowly so I wouldn't be expected to add anything further to the conversation.

Mother, now done with me, refilled her wineglass and straightened in her chair. She took a healthy sip and smoothed out a wrinkle in the tablecloth with her milky hand. She addressed Father: "I spoke to your sister-in-law today."

"Did you?" Father continued to eviscerate his tenderloin.

"I did, yes. John is taking Sarah and the children to Aruba for Christmas this year."

"Well, good for John."

"Yes, it is good for John. Good for all of them, really. I imagine it must be nice to spend the winter somewhere warm."

"Hmmph."

Mother, unsatisfied with Father's response, turned back to me. "Your Uncle John takes Sarah and the children someplace every winter, you know. Last year they went to Provence." She continued before I could respond. "Yes, every year they choose someplace they haven't been and go on holiday for a few weeks." Mother drained her glass. "They must be doing very well."

"They both work," Father said through a mouthful of beef.

"Oh, hardly. From what I understand, Sarah only consults on one or two designs a year." Mother turned back to me. "Your Uncle John is very successful, you know."

I used my fork to trace figure eights in my gravy and shifted in my chair. My chest tightened and I felt my bowels begin to percolate.

Father's knuckles grew white around his cutlery. "I guess you married the wrong brother then."

Undaunted, Mother reached again for the bottle of cabernet sauvignon and filled her glass to the top. I watched the meniscus arc over the rim. She raised it and drank expertly, not a drop spilled. "Well, Edward, you certainly found the money to take that little tramp abroad." Mother leaned back triumphantly and took a gulp.

Father pounded the table with both fists. A lone pea jumped off his plate and rolled across the table, stopping just shy of my hand. "That was business, Shirley." A glob of mashed potato dropped from his mouth back to the plate. "Is that how you want to vacation, huh? Milwaukee in October? Christ."

The little tramp in question was Belinda, Father's assistant for well over a decade. Belinda was in her mid-sixties and clearly uninterested in men, which I had confirmed by regularly running into her and her partner at the coffee shop near my apartment. Arbitration can be a form of meddling, so I chose to keep this information silent and instead stared at the rogue pea. It had a dimple on one side. I closed my eyes for a moment and pictured myself shrinking down, small enough to curl up in the pea's cavity, like a little beanbag chair.

"I've seen the way she looks at you, Edward, and the way she dresses, her tits out for everyone to see." Mother's voice dropped a notch. "She wants our money."

Father, jaw taut, glowered across the table. He leaned forward, dragging his shirtsleeve through the gravy pooled on his plate. "But we need that money, Shirley. It's the only thing keeping your face together."

Mother gasped and then grinned viciously, her hands gathering fistfuls of pristine tablecloth. She leaned in, pearls swinging like a pendulum over her untouched plate, and inhaled deeply, preparing for her next volley.

"May I be excused?" I asked, unnoticed, and removed myself from the table. I plodded out of the room and up the stairs, voices rising behind me. Instinctively, I retreated to the guest room, which had still been my bedroom only a few years before. I entered the ensuite bathroom, dropped my pants, and expelled a sluice of diarrhea into the bowl. After the spasms ceased, I continued to sit, meditating on the straight lines of the face cloth and hand towel perfectly hung on the bar across from me. I tried to work on my Coherent Breathing, five breaths per minute like Dr. Matthews instructed me, but the foulness of the room made it unpleasant.

I washed my hands with a small, strong-smelling soap in the shape of a Scottish terrier, then dried them and let the hand towel fall to the floor. I left the bathroom and lay down on the bed before returning and re-hanging the towel at the proper angle. Back on the bed, I pressed my face into the covers and arched a cloud-like pillow over my head, effectively muting the sounds that clawed through the hardwood below, and repeated my mantras. "I deserve all that is good. I will accept the things I cannot change." The goose down absorbed the words. "I am free. I am free. I am free."

PEOPLE USED TO MISTAKE Paddy and me for twins, he being younger by less than a year. As I watched him joke with his friends, his arm carelessly thrown across the shoulder of the girl in sunglasses, I realized there'd be no making that mistake anymore. Paddy was nothing like the pale, doughy boy I'd grown up with. He did yoga now. He'd gotten Lasik surgery and grown sideburns. Paddy pulled the redhead in closer and nipped at her neck, making her giggle and push him away in mock shock. The party was supposed to be for me, but Paddy took centre stage.

I begged off early, despite my brother's admonitions that I not be "such a stiff." I wanted to get to the drugstore near my hotel before it closed, to get my M&Ms—magnesium for anxiety, melatonin for sleep. A little joke between Dr. Matthews and me.

I AWOKE TO A crash and the sound of heavy footfalls on the front steps. I looked out over the driveway and watched as Father struggled with his navy jacket, one sleeve trailing behind him. He reached his Mercedes and tried to open the driver's door, fingers flailing at the handle. I squinted hard and allowed myself the fantasy that the waving sleeve was a tail and the figure below was not my father but rather a clumsy blue cartoon cat who wanted to drive. I had a little giggle to myself until a bottle exploded against the trunk and the illusion broke. Green glass confetti flew across the bricks.

Mother staggered into view, screeching and brandishing another empty wine bottle. Father, however, was surprisingly quick for his size and managed to get his arm into the sleeve and drop into the car seat before she had time to hurl it. Mother abandoned the bottle and lurched forward, heels catching on the bricks, grabbing at the still-open door. As she shrieked, she gripped the car door with her left hand and the seatback with her right, trying to pry the door further open. Father, turned awkwardly in his seat, had both hands on the inside handle as he tried to yank it closed. He hammered at the pedals with his feet, which caused the Mercedes to jump ahead a foot or two at a time. Mother's bun came unfurled.

I turned away from the scene and looked back at the bed for a moment, that seductive nest, before continuing out of the room, along the hall, down the stairs, across the foyer and past the remains of a potted fern slumped against the doorframe, and out through the front door. I reached the steps in time to witness Father, with one final courageous heave, slamming the door shut. Mother produced an unearthly howl but continued to hold fast, clinging to the side of the vehicle as it careened around the driveway. She pounded her bony fist against the roof and followed Father as he attempted the three-point turn necessary to escape. The Mercedes's back fender crunched into the door of my Nissan, and then Father gunned it, knocking Mother free and leaving her to roll across the ground as he disappeared down the driveway, dust and glass in his wake.

Mother lay face down, arms tucked to her chest. I could hear her moaning, low and soft, as I approached and gingerly knelt, pulling her onto her back. Her legs were dotted with small rocks and green crystals, spots of blood blooming through her nylons, her skirt hiked embarrassingly high. Her blouse was untucked and matted with sweat and dirt. As I pulled her hands apart, blood spouted forth and a spray leapt up to coat her neck and pearls.

THE MORNING AFTER THE party, Paddy, deeply hungover, had picked me up at my hotel. On the way to the airport, he'd delivered what I supposed was his version of an intervention, a little brotherly tough love.

"Fucking hell, Mitch, why do you do it to yourself?" he said. "Every time I see you, it's like you're shrinking. The Murderess is going to keep killing every shred of joy in you until there's nothing left. I mean, you're never going to get a girlfriend if you're still suckling at that dusty teat. Her milk is acid."

"Don't say that, Patrick. You just don't understand."

"The Heap probably hasn't said fifteen words to you in the last year," he said. "That's neglect, at best."

"They're of a different generation. It's unfair to expect them to be as gooey as everyone else these days."

"Enabler." At the stoplight, he turned to me. "Listen, Mitch, why don't you just come and live with me here. The city's booming. And the Rockies are basically the Iron Curtain; you'd never hear from them again."

As the light turned and we started moving again, I said, "Victoria's my home. Someone has to be there for them; they're becoming so fragile in their old age."

WHEN THE ER DOCTOR realized I brought in Mother without her finger, he sent me back to the house to look for it. In the waning light, I searched the driveway and turned up nothing, save for a single heeled shoe tucked under a rhodo. I drove the streets of Oak Bay, hunting for Father.

The Mercedes wasn't parked at the Yacht Club or Father's office, so I directed my dented little car into the lot behind The Fox and Pheasant, one of the city's last bastions of idealized Britishness.

Father's car sat in the farthest spot, a spattering of blood dried to the doorframe. Father reclined in his seat, cigarette burning between his lips, windows rolled up. I pulled at the handle. Father started, sending an avalanche of ash down his chest, and stared at me uncomprehendingly for a moment before unlocking the door. I opened it, gripped him by the lapels and, with some difficulty, hauled his dense body out of the car.

Father inhaled deeply, then shot smoke through his nostrils. "What is it, Mitchell? What do you want now?" He reached back to scratch at his rear.

I knelt again and ran my fingers along the carpet under the seat, then took his lighter from the centre console and waved it back and forth, close to the pedals, in the crease of the seat, above the cup holder. Father stood mute, observing me as the smoke burnt down between his fingers.

I stood and took Father by the shoulders, digging my hands deep into the pockets of his navy jacket with the gold crest. In his left pocket, I grasped something sticky and retracted my hand. We both stared for a few seconds at my closed fist. Father's eyes went wide and he stumbled back against the hood as I opened my hand to reveal one white, roughly severed finger, French-manicured nail intact.

Father turned and splashed vomit across the hood of the Merc. All that expensive beef.

FATHER DROVE HOME to collect some items for Mother's stay at Vic General and returned looking old and shaken. The selections he made, stuffed into a grocery bag, were motley: a silk scarf, two bras, a pair of slacks, a black dress, lipstick, socks. At one point, I stepped into Mother's room to find him busy at the basin, scrubbing the splatter from her pearls. I could hear him grunting from the exertion needed for such a delicate operation. I backed out through the door without a sound.

Late that night, Father sat across from me in the waiting area, staring down at an ancient magazine unopened in his lap. He succumbed to the scoop of the vinyl chair and slumped forward, burdened by his own mammoth frame. Father looked up from his magazine to see me observing him. I reminded myself to ask HR if my insurance would cover increasing my appointments with Dr. Matthews to twice weekly. "Don't stare at me all goggle-eyed, Mitchell." Father kept fingering a small bloodstain on the outside of his jacket pocket. "You look like a blasted grouper." He opened and closed his mouth a few times to demonstrate.

"Excuse me, Father." I followed a line of green tape

down the hallway to Mother's room. I entered and sat in the half-light of the corner. Mother lay in a drugged sleep. The equipment that surrounded her hushed and beeped softly. I closed my eyes and envisioned these sounds as coming from a gently glowing, benevolent orb that hovered over me, soothing. I pictured it encircling me, calming and caring, until Mother began to stir.

"Mitchell, bring me a mirror." Her voice was hoarse.

"Not to worry, Mother, it was just your hand," I whispered. "They've managed to reattach your finger."

"What did I just say?" Mother slapped at the bed control until she was upright.

I located Mother's purse in the closet and fished around until I found her compact. She flicked it open with a nail on her free hand. I realized that I'd never seen Mother without makeup before — she was incredibly pale then, even by her usual bleached-bone standards, her forehead lined and scratched from the tussle. While she scanned her reflection, Mother's face became grim and tight. "My God, I'm disfigured." She pawed at her hair with her bandaged hand, jerking the IV stand around like a marionette. "The doctors will think I'm a guttersnipe." As she began to sob, I pushed the nurse's call button and excused myself from the room.

ONCE I GOT OFF the phone with Dr. Matthews, I called my brother.

"Someone's going to end up dead, Mitch. Probably you."

"No, Patrick, don't you see? This is exactly what they, what we all, needed. Mother and Father have finally reached their lowest ebb—it's an uphill climb from now on. And Dr. Matthews says that, by witnessing the whole affair, I've inadvertently experienced a form of immersion therapy. I've immersed myself in the very sort of thing that's been at the pinnacle of my fear hierarchy all these years. Everything will be different now."

"What the fuck are you even talking about? They're not—"

I lay the phone down and let Paddy express his useless anger.

A FEW WEEKS LATER, after assembling a teak patio set for the upstairs veranda, I again sat in the dining room, keen to eat. Father stood at the sideboard, carving a haunch of venison, while Mother asked me a number of questions about work, childhood friends, my love life, my brother. As she sat, Mother reached over and placed her hand on Father's hip. Her middle finger jutted out abruptly, the jagged scar red and puffy. On the next finger was a gleaming gold ring, a fat emerald clustered with diamonds. It was a very becoming and, no doubt, generous gift.

We ate in a comfortable sort of silence, and I wished Paddy was there, if for no other reason than to see that change was possible, that it really was dimmest just before the light. As Dr. Matthews put it, sometimes through trauma comes progress. Yes, the past had been unsettling in some ways, but look at the advancement it had brought.

Mother laid her silverware on the side of her plate and straightened in her chair. Her hand rose up to adjust her pearls. She reached for the bottle and topped up her glass. Father continued to enjoy his mountain of mashed potato with his customary gusto. Mother, a smile tugging at the corners of her mouth, addressed him: "I spoke to your sister-in-law today."

I am free.

"Did you?"

I am free.

"I did, yes."

I am free.

Registry

MARLON SAT HUNCHED ON a plastic milk crate in the storeroom, knees bracketing a dented cardboard box. He dipped his long fingers inside and removed a wineglass from between the flimsy dividers, tilting it back and forth in the light, before it was deemed acceptable and placed in a row of others on a low shelf to his right. Every fourth or fifth one was defective in some way, the glass bubbled or warped, stems crooked or truncated, lips chipped; these he set in a neat huddle on the floor to his left, to be later removed from inventory. Marlon hummed a working song as he sorted.

The door swung open, and Ruby's head poked around the corner. "She's back."

Marlon stopped mid-hum and looked up. "Who's back?"

Ruby rolled her eyes. "Holy duh, Marlon, you know

who." She jutted out her chin and clenched her jaw, spoke in a faux–country club accent. "The fiancée." Her hand rose to stroke an imaginary strand of pearls around her neck. "Oh, you haven't heard? I'm engaged to my fiancé. My fiancé."

Before Marlon could chide her for speaking too loudly and disrespectfully, Ruby said, "She's your weird customer. You deal with her," and disappeared from view.

Once he was sure Ruby was gone, Marlon stood, undid and retied his apron, and straightened his collar. He reached up and pulled one of the copper skillets from the top shelf, wrestled it out of its protective brown paper and inspected his face in the pan's gleaming underside. He removed a fleck of cilantro from between his teeth, then returned the pan to its wrapping and stepped through the doorway and on to the sales floor. At the sound of his footfalls, a woman standing alone near the cash desk turned and smiled, while Ruby hovered near the wok display, an unused dust cloth limp in her hand.

Marlon spoke as he approached: "And how is the soon-to-be-former Miss Higgins today?"

The woman giggled, her hands leaping up to cover her mouth. "I'm well, Marlon," she said. "Call me Glenda, remember?"

"Of course, Glenda. I'm just being silly. What's on the agenda for today?"

Glenda steepled her hands in front of her chest and grew

serious. "Well, Marlon, I'm a little confused about knives. Do you have a few minutes?"

"Of course I do, Glenda; I always have time," Marlon said. "Let me just dig out the wedding registry, and I'll meet you at the knife cabinet in two shakes."

As Glenda turned away, Marlon looked over to where Ruby stood gawking and made a wiping motion with his hand. Ruby again rolled her eyes—her primary method of communication—and petulantly began to dust.

MARLON AND GLENDA STOOD in front of the glass case of knives, his shrine to culinary engineering. Though he did not own the store and simply managed it on behalf of the frequently absent owner, Marlon took great pride in the cabinet. He kept the keys safely in his apron pocket and rarely granted the rest of the staff access. Only the previous day, he had dragged the dodgy wooden ladder out of the storeroom and risked a broken back in order to adjust the track lighting on the ceiling around the cabinet, angling the bulbs so that the light glinted off the blades in a way he thought both subtle and divine. Marlon noted that Glenda also appeared to view the cabinet with due reverence and that her questions were thoughtful and many, which allowed him the opportunity to speak at length about the difference between Japanese and German angling, the benefits of molybdenum, the importance of balance. Glenda nodded continuously as he spoke.

Marlon turned to her. "Does your fiancé cook much?"

Glenda's nodding grew vigorous. "Oh, yes," she said. "David's an amazing cook. He makes the most incredible breakfasts. Also, dinners. Lunches on the weekend. Brunch."

"Excellent. And would you describe his cooking as more Asian- or European-influenced?"

"Well, we're both mad about Thai. In fact, we're going there for our honeymoon. To Thailand, I mean. Did you know you can take cooking classes there, right on the beach? It's supposed to be amazing. Anyway, at home, David mostly cooks European. He's very accomplished in Spanish and French cooking."

"I see." Marlon turned to regard the knives. "And would you say he's a large man, your David?"

Glenda's brow creased. "Why do you ask?"

"What I mean is, does he have large hands? Presumably, you'll want knives that both of you will use."

"Oh, I understand." Glenda thought for a moment. "David is tall. But he has an architect's hands. Slender, for sketching. Like yours."

"Excellent," Marlon repeated. "You see, Glenda, the most important consideration when selecting a blade is that it feel good in your hand. It doesn't matter how well a knife is made; if you don't enjoy holding it, then it's not the right one for you." He leaned forward and plucked a knife from the magnetic rack. Marlon grasped the spine with the fingers of his other hand and held the handle out for Glenda to take. "Because you have such fine hands, as does David from what you've said, then I would recommend something like this."

Glenda hesitated. Her hand hovered a few inches away before she cautiously reached forward to take the handle. She held the knife awkwardly, with the same fear and awe that Marlon noticed in so many novice cooks, and brought it down through the air a few times, as though to clumsily hack through an unseen squash.

Marlon continued: "Now, the standard chef's knife is eight inches; this one is six, which I personally prefer. I find you get much more control with a shorter blade, and control is vital. It's not the cheapest knife, to be certain, but well worth the money in my opinion."

Glenda appraised the weight, letting it bounce a little in her palm. "It's perfect," she said. "I love it, Marlon. My fiancé will love it."

"Shall I add it to the list?"

Glenda blushed and looked to the floor. "Yes," she said. "Please do." She handed the knife back.

Marlon pinched the blade between his thumb and pointer finger and laid it down on a shelf next to the wedding registry. He opened and flipped through the archaic vinyl binder until he came to a tab that read "Higgins, Glenda and David Carmichael." His finger trailed down the list of selected items until he reached a blank slot. In his meticulous script, he wrote out a description of the knife, copying the serial number printed in tiny numerals near the bolster, as Glenda watched over his shoulder. Marlon apologized again for the outdatedness of the store's registry system.

Glenda shook her head. "The personal touch is so often lost, nowadays."

Marlon agreed wholeheartedly.

HER VISITS INCREASED OVER the next few weeks, Glenda coming in to discuss with Marlon the pros and cons of aluminum vs. steel bakeware or the proper use of a non-stick pan or the questionable necessity of owning a soup tureen, each time adding one or two choice pieces to the slowly expanding registry. She appeared, uniformly alone, in the evenings or on weekends, when he was sure to be there to guide her. Ruby, whom Marlon distrusted to accomplish anything without his direct supervision, was regularly present to acknowledge Glenda with her trademark monosyllabic greeting and shallow, insincere smile.

One evening, after he'd escorted Glenda to the door and bid her goodnight, Marlon turned to find Ruby staring at him. "Oh. My. Christ. You're into that woman, aren't you? You're hot for the fiancée."

"What?" Marlon said. "That's ridiculous. I'm just being polite. Which, incidentally, you might try yourself sometime."

Ruby's eyes narrowed. "I don't know, Marl. You're looking more and more like my dad after Mom left him—like a sad, horny old dad. Eww."

"Honestly, Ruby. Would it kill you to have a little professionalism?" Marlon shook his head and walked away.

"Well, I'm just saying. Even you could probably do better," she called after him. Marlon didn't respond.

Protestations aside, Marlon did think of Glenda often. As the fuss of the holiday shopping season melted into the stillness of late winter, and since the store was located in an unlauded corner of the city, business became glacially slow. Glenda, with her intelligent queries and mutual love of high-quality cookware, gave Marlon a focal point, a receptacle for his oft-wasted knowledge. He constantly reassessed his mental list of cooking and baking essentials, keen to formulate his next gem of advice for her. Sometimes, he thought of the two of them cooking together in his kitchen. Sometimes, he thought about the way the top button of her blouse strained against the swell of her chest.

During the most recent visit, Marlon allowed himself a question he knew bordered on rude: "Tell me, Glenda, when will David be able to join us? I would love to put a face to the name."

Glenda shook her head. "It'll be a while, I'm afraid. David's been called away to a conference. In Berlin."

"Another conference? He must spend more time in a plane than at home. How glamorous."

"He's kind of a hot commodity right now." She shrugged. "You know what they say: it's hell to be popular."

"I wouldn't know." Marlon offered a smile he hoped read as self-deprecating. "Still, it must be difficult at times. To be alone so often while he's away."

"It's something you just get used to." Her smile brightened. "Now, what do you recommend in the way of spatulas?"

AT HOME THAT NIGHT, in his small, clean apartment in another unexceptional part of the city, Marlon prepared his dinner. He cut juliennes of orange pepper, adding them to a pan already sizzling with garlic, shallots, and chorizo. While they softened, he cracked an egg into a small pot of roiling water and brushed a slice of French bread with olive oil before placing it in a skillet to brown. As he worked, Marlon alternately hummed his atonal tune and spoke aloud to himself, constructing one half of a conversation he intended to trigger soon.

After a few minutes, he placed the slice of crisped bread onto a white plate, covered it evenly with the cooked chorizo and peppers, and topped it with his soft-poached egg. Before he carried the plate to the kitchen table, he returned to the cutting board and chopped a small mound of Italian parsley for garnish and colour. Marlon tucked his chair tight to the table's edge and slid his knife through the yolk, allowing it to sauce the dish before he dug in. Between mouthfuls, he continued his half of the conversation and tailored his speech to the imagined responses: the desired tone was earnest with a soupçon of playfulness. He addressed his comments to a space above the unused plate and cutlery he'd set at the opposite, empty side of the table.

THE FOLLOWING DAY, GLENDA arrived at the store, alone. The two of them exchanged pleasantries and discussed what each had had for dinner the previous night. Both agreed that Marlon's sausage-and-egg-on-toast was the perfect meal for a chilly night, elegant in its simplicity. He slowly steered Glenda through the aisles as they spoke until they arrived in the cleaning and storage section, the dimmest and least-loved area of the store. They were the only two on the floor. Marlon talked about springform pans with such mounting fervour that Glenda finally commented.

"Are you okay, Marlon?"

"None of the peppermills we received today grind properly and I don't think you should marry David," Marlon blurted, almost shouting. The air around them stiffened as each grew aware of the other's breathing; Glenda's mouth hung open slightly. Marlon's brain scrambled to retrieve the vocabulary of the exchange he'd envisioned the night before. He finally settled on "I'm so sorry."

Glenda's mouth began to move again. "Why would you even say that?" Her round cheeks were red.

Marlon swallowed hard. "It's just that you're always here alone," he began. "You've been coming in for weeks and weeks, putting all this work into choosing items. Into building a beautiful kitchen, a home, and David's never once come with you. You deserve an equal partner, someone who embraces your interests."

He took a step closer to Glenda, a clear violation of his own rule about personal space. "It's awful to be alone." He reached his hand out towards her.

Glenda took an equivalent step back, her eyes welling, before she spun and hastened from the store. On her way out, she passed Ruby, just back from another smoke break; Ruby held the door open as Glenda pushed past without a word.

Marlon stood silently among the dish-drying racks and scrub brushes, the worst version of his intended conversation now realized, as Ruby dumped her purse on the counter and scanned the store for his presence. She caught him watching Glenda's figure recede through the window and called out, "Did she finally lose her shit? See, I told you. That woman is so fucking pathetic. Totally damaged."

"Don't say that," Marlon hissed. He strode to the counter and jabbed his finger at her. "You don't know anything about her. Her life is complicated."

Ruby shook her head pitifully. "I know you have this freakish dedication to customer service and everything, Marlon, but sometimes the customer is fucking crazy," she said. "I mean, there's probably no fiancé, right?"

"What do you mean?" Marlon stared at her for a moment. "Yes, there is. His name is David."

"Fucking hell, think about it, Marl. She's what, forty-five years old? She looks like a librarian—and not the sexy kind. I'm sure she's got, like, a million cats."

"She's not a librarian," Marlon said. "She's an actuary."

"Well, whatever—she dresses like a cat lady. And yet, somehow, she has this globe-trotting architect boyfriend—who no one's ever seen, by the way—who also happens to be a gourmet cook? Like, where would they even meet?"

Marlon tried to recall the last few weeks' worth of conversations with Glenda. "I don't know," he conceded. "But what about the ring? She has an engagement ring."

"Holy shit, you're naive." Ruby held up her hands to display a dozen rings spread across the pair. "She's probably registered at half the stores in town. It would be kind of depressing if it wasn't totally batshit." She clomped back to the storeroom, her gigantic purse jangling, and left Marlon to stand alone at the counter.

MARLON DRIFTED THROUGH THE rest of his shift — he counted and recounted a stack of porcelain ramekins, turned the French ovens so the labels all faced the same direction, organized the drawer of stationery supplies under the counter — while Ruby continued to talk at him. He finally offered to let her leave early; she was out the door almost before his sentence was complete. Marlon stood alone again at the counter and let the silence of the store calm his doubts before he allowed himself the minor indiscretion of shutting off the bank of lights above the entrance and locking the door at five minutes to the hour.

Once the store was darkened, he stood in the glow of the lit cabinet. Marlon slid the ring of keys out of his apron pocket and opened the glass door. He let his fingers lightly bump along the rows of parallel handles until he reached the six-inch chef's. He lifted it from the bar and found its empty box in the storeroom, then carried it to the front counter, where he scraped the price tag off with a fingernail. Marlon dampened a cloth with rubbing alcohol and rubbed the handle in tight circles until all the remaining sticker residue was gone. He wiped the blade down with a chamois to remove his fingerprints, studied it for nicks or scratches, checked the security of the rivets. Satisfied, Marlon placed it in the box, careful to close the tabs with enough pressure so they didn't crease unduly, and scanned it with the barcode reader. He paid the $189.12 with his debit card and without deducting his usual staff discount—an anonymous transaction. Marlon fished the tattered binder from the shelf below and flipped until he came to the tab that read "Higgins, Glenda and David Carmichael." His finger snaked down the column of entries until he found the listing for the knife and drew a neat line through it, marking the day's date and entering a question mark in the box for the purchaser's initials.

Before he wrapped the box in plain brown paper, he slid in a small envelope with a card that read: "To Glenda and David, May you always exist in each other's hearts, Happy Cooking, your friend, M."

Marlon copied the address from the registry to the brown paper in his immaculate hand, placed the package in the stack of items to be mailed out, and sat down to begin his paperwork.

Do the Donna

DONNA-MARIE NEVER DOES THIS. But it's her last night in the biggest city she's ever been to, last night of her biggest conference and trade show, her first trade show as the president of a self-started holistic dog food company. Her suitcase sits on the bed of her room upstairs, almost packed—the rectangular Pet Benefit sign the conference provided folded and tucked inside as a souvenir—and all the samples she brought from home, all the pamphlets, all the key chains she had specially made are gone, so she doesn't have to pay extra baggage on the return. There is a fat stack of business cards in her purse, interest from distributors as far away as Mexico. She takes her third gin-and-ginger from the bartender and crosses the hotel's lower-level ballroom to the edge of the dance floor. She watches conference attendees move their bodies, nods her head to the music, swivels at the waist a little. Someone waves to her, and she waves back.

She hadn't expected the camaraderie. The other pet food reps have been terrific, a little family emerging from the neighbouring booths, always someone to watch her stuff when she needed a bathroom break, genuine interest in her product, in her story. After she complained how Hooch, her Boston Terrier, woke her up every morning nosing his food bowl across the tile of her kitchen, the rep from Thank Dog gave her a new dish — on the house — with a textured, no-slip rubber base. Yesterday, Kathy from Purrfect Pelt brought Donna-Marie a muffin, a good one from a proper bakery, with blackberries and a streusel top. Just excellent, like-minded people.

At fifty-six, Donna-Marie isn't the oldest one here. She's not the most awkwardly dressed, either, everyone in poly-blend khakis or promotional tees or skirts wrinkled from three days living out of a duffel bag. When the DJ takes the mic and shouts, "Canadian Pet Food Manufacturers Association, let's make some noooooooise!" and the crowd cheers, it should be embarrassing, but it's not. The DJ knows these people; there's not been a single song that Donna-Marie hasn't at least heard before. She closes her eyes for a few beats and lets the lights strobe against her face.

IN HIS TOO-BIG UNIFORM shirt with the bowling pins on the back, Mickey wasn't cool. He wasn't particularly attractive either: lank brown hair tucked behind his ears, reed thin, weirdly long fingers. But he could be kind of funny sometimes and, at eighteen—almost two full years younger than Donna—was eager to impress. The two of them worked at Lakefield Lanes, Donna positioned behind the shoe counter, Mickey at the concession.

Several times a night, he would abandon his station to bring her a corndog or some red licorice or, if it was quiet and near close, a beer poured into a soda cup. Ever since the roller rink had opened, no young people came to the alley anymore, so she accepted his company, a welcome break from all the old men. Sometimes, if it was totally dead, they would bowl a game without keeping score. Both were equally bad at their jobs.

WHEN DONNA-MARIE OPENS HER eyes, Gord from the brine shrimp-cube stall is reaching out for her, his grey ponytail falling forward as he leans down to grab her wrist. She laughs and lets herself be pulled onto the dance floor. Gord drops his hand from her arm to her waist and gives Donna-Marie what she knows are meant to be sex-eyes. What he lacks in subtlety, Gord also lacks in self-consciousness, bringing his knees up high as he dances, arms splayed out, his tan deep against the white golf shirt with the prawn insignia on the breast pocket. Her sister had told her that out-of-town conferences were basically pick-up free-for-alls, and Donna-Marie had scoffed, but she can see how it could easily happen, how it might be happening now. She slips out of her flats and hooks them on the fingers of her non-drink hand, twists her nyloned feet on the sticky floor. After being absorbed with work for so long, weeks at a time alone in her kitchen with bowls of raw meat, months of research and trials, it feels good to let go a bit.

DONNA THOUGHT IT WAS sort of cute that Mickey had such an obvious crush on her, but she had an off-again, on-again with Brandt, who was twenty-five and wore a leather vest. Mickey was fine, really, but never a contender, not in that way.

He had a band — The Governors General — and sometimes brought in lyrics for Donna to read, written neatly in a lined Hilroy notebook. She didn't know how to respond to words like *I saw you look through me / to something better on the other side* but recognized that Mickey was giving her access to his whole self, which allowed her in turn to talk freely about the things she never talked about. How she was doomed to never see the world, like her parents. How her acne scars would never fade. How Brandt might be biding his time with her until something fresher came along.

DONNA-MARIE DANCES IN A sloppy circle with Gord, and Kit and Crystal from Little Critters, and some other friendly faces. High-fives are given, butts get shook. First, Gord's thigh rubs against hers, then Crystal's. Someone's drink sloshes onto her calf, turns her nylons spongey, but she doesn't care. In the moment, she wishes she had spent less time trying to lower the pH level in her Venison Plus for Aging Dogs and more time dancing. She loves the way the bass makes her lungs compress.

As the last number starts to fade out, DJ Jimbo shouts, "Let's take this party baaaaaack!" and the opening drum-beats of the next song come skittering from the speakers. Around her, people hoot. Gord gives a fist pump. The song's twitchy guitar squiggles out and the propulsive bass line chugs along before the vocals kick in.

> *Hey there tiger, in your kitten heels*
> *You raise me up when you get down*
> *Bend those knees, twist your wrists*
> *Ooh baby, you know I like it like this*
> *You just know that I am gonna*
> *Go crazy, when you do the Donna*

ONE NIGHT, 11:30, MICKEY turned off the hot dog roller and came over to lean his back against the shoe counter, elbows propped on the countertop, looking out over the empty lanes. "I'm working on some killer material for the band," he said. "You should come check us out tomorrow."

"Oh, yeah?" Donna continued to douse shoes with anti-fungal spray. "Maybe."

"Cool, cool. We practise, like, at least three times a week. Our new bassist is totally ace."

She nodded, lined the size 10s up in neat pairs. "Let me think about it."

"Sure, no big deal." Mickey whistled some tune for a few seconds then turned to face her. "Hey, what about Wednesday? There's a new Gene Hackman flick at the Brighton. Some of the guys are going, if you want to join."

"I'm pretty busy Wednesday. Why don't you ask Stacey? She's probably not doing anything."

"I don't want to go with Stacey," he said, his voice sombre. "I want to go with you."

She looked up from the shoes and saw how strained his face was, his long fingers suddenly tensed along the counter's edge. "That's sweet, Mickey, it really is. But you know I'm involved." She almost reached out to put her hand on the back of his but didn't.

"Right." Mickey laughed, once. "Brandt."

Donna frowned. "Why do you say it like that? Did you hear something?"

Mickey shook his head. "No, no, I just...nothing." He looked around, then leaned in and dropped his voice low. "Let me get you off, then. You don't have to do anything back, I swear." He held up his hand in a shaky Boy Scout salute.

Donna stared across the counter at him, tried to evaluate his seriousness. And she thought about it for a second, she really did—sitting on the lid of the staff toilet, pants and underwear still hooked on an ankle, Mickey's peachfuzz moustache pushed between her legs, his hand gripped to her thigh. The image made her feel a little ill.

"Please," he said. "I know I'd be good at it."

"Ew. No."

Mickey slunk back across the thin carpeting and stood slumped against the popcorn machine until their shifts were over.

GORD MOUTHS ALONG WITH the words, gives finger guns, thrusts his groin in her direction. Over his shoulder, Donna-Marie can see Kathy reeling towards them. Kathy clasps her hands to Donna-Marie's shoulder, blasts boozy breath into her ear. "This song is like your name!" The dance circle clusters closer around her as the chorus kicks in.

D-d-d-d-d-d-do the Donna
You can do it, I know that you wanna
D-d-d-d-d-d-do the Donna
Swallow me down, just like a piranha

Donna-Marie's dancing falters, her sense of rhythm out of sync, and then stops, limbs wooden. She clutches the gin to her chest to keep it from dropping while her shoes hang limp from her other hand. Her heart is a stress ball squeezed in a cold fist.

AFTER HER REJECTION OF his come-on, Mickey became good at his job. He stopped bringing her Red-Hots and mostly kept to his side of the alley. He was polite enough but never showed her his lyric book or set up a lane for them again. Once, he posted a flyer for his band's first-ever public gig on the community board next to the shoe station but didn't even look in Donna's direction.

A few months later, Donna's cousin Janet announced her plan to move to Edmonton and invited Donna to join her. Brandt had moved on to someone else — unceremoniously dumping her on a Wednesday night after the two of them had made out in his Datsun at the foot of her parents' driveway — so Donna shrugged and said sure. She gave her notice at work and didn't say anything about it to Mickey.

Janet rented them a small apartment off the main drag, and Donna found her way into the provincial government's secretarial pool. She worked long days, had drinks on Fridays with the other gals, went on a few lukewarm dates with a veterinarian named Jim, who helped her pick out a dog from the SPCA, a mutt she named Rascal. Within three years, she'd put together enough for a down payment on a small bungalow with a fenced backyard in a quiet neighbourhood.

She was still unpacking her boxes when she heard from Stacey, her first phone call in her first home. "The house sounds real nice and everything," Stacey said, "but have you heard the song yet?"

* * *

What's up sugar, what's on your mind?
Open your mouth, so we can both find out
Hey b-b-baby, I know you got needs
Come closer, let me plant that seed
You say that you don't wanna
Go crazy, but then you do the Donna

Donna-Marie pushes her way off the dance floor, places her glass on the carpet near the wall, tries to remember which of the darkened bar tables she left her purse on.

FOR MONTHS, THE SONG stayed near the top of the charts, and for months Donna suffered through phone calls from anonymous men who claimed to know her, who described the things they wanted to do to her or have her do to them, from old girlfriends wanting to know if Mickey was as good in the sack as they'd heard, concerned calls from her guileless parents about the rumours that circulated at the Legion. There were other Donnas from her town, but everyone seemed to know it was about her. She once received a Christmas card in the mail, with a graphically detailed pencil drawing inside of a woman being impaled through the neck by a penis. The card had no signature or return address, but the face on the woman was a close approximation of hers. She had deadbolts installed on her doors and changed her phone number. Donna stopped going home, instead footing the bill to fly her parents out to visit.

The song never seemed to die. In the decades after its release, it showed up in a commercial for a car company, as the basis for a sketch on a popular late-night comedy show, on the soundtrack for a film by a hot, up-and-coming direc-tor, always re-emerging just as she was ready to forget about it. She stopped going to clubs after years of men dancing at her, trying to use the song as a seduction, blissfully ignorant to the irony that it *was* about her, a puerile number-one smash hit about a blowjob she never gave to some guy she worked with for a summer. She stopped wearing makeup and cut her hair short to distance herself from the image of her she thought the song projected. She never listened to the radio, never watched music videos, but still somehow heard it in the week she buried Rascal, heard it while she stood in line to submit her application to business school, heard it the same day she finalized her divorce from Jim.

Should she have been nicer to Mickey, shown more interest? Would that have made a difference? Maybe she should have leaned into it, outed herself, and found a way to capitalize. She tried to convince herself that she should be thankful for the song's existence — that it helped build her successes by making her take herself more seriously — and longed to achieve some kind of playful, or even grudging, acceptance. But she couldn't seem to get there. The one time she'd broken down — actually broken down, sobbing in a food court while the song played on hidden overhead speakers — and tried to explain the song to Jim, what a violation it was, how undermining, he'd laughed and used it to fuel his claim that Donna had no sense of humour. He popped another french fry in his mouth and absently tapped his hand against the plastic table in time to the beat while she wiped her face with a napkin.

SHE NEVER SAW MICKEY again in person—he reportedly moved the band to Los Angeles as soon as the song hit big stateside—but did see him on television. The first time was during the song's initial run of popularity, by accident, on a British variety show she sometimes tuned in to. She missed the band's performance but caught the beginning of Mickey's interview with the show's host, a leering, older Englishman with gigantic lapels. The host asked about the song's inspiration.

"I guess you could say it's a tribute to all the girls who never said no." Mickey looked the same, straight hair to his shoulder, but he'd become suave somehow, rakish. He was still lanky, but he was outfitted in clothes that fit. Tight trousers and a skinny tie under a brown leather vest.

"So, is there a Donna?" the host asked.

Mickey looked directly into the camera. "A gentleman never tells." He winked.

It felt like Mickey was winking right at her through the screen, an acknowledgement that she was somehow complicit in the joke. Donna turned off the TV and cried by herself in her little house.

DONNA-MARIE WEAVES THROUGH a phalanx of backlit silhouettes, around another tall man drunkenly shouting the song's chorus, finds her purse, only to realize she no longer has her shoes. She searches for an exit sign, but it's a huge room and there are red lights everywhere. Her logic centre tells her she's overreacting, but fuck that, she is on the verge of hyperventilation, full kaleidoscopic panic.

The flashing lights make faces hard to read, and she wants to yank on someone's sleeve to help her get out but doesn't want to embarrass herself in front of these people. She can't, not after she's quit her comfortable middle-management job to gamble on Pet Benefit and sold her house for less than asking in order to rent a place with a garage that fits three deep-freezes.

Donna-Marie just wants dogs to lead healthier lives.

THE SECOND TIME SHE saw Mickey on TV, intentional and nearly two decades after the song broke, was as part of a documentary series called *One-Hit Wonders: What the $#!& Happened?* She poured herself a glass of red and lowered herself into her TV chair, patted her lap for Cinnamon, her Sheltie, to jump up. She turned the set on and waited for it to begin. Mickey appeared alone in front of the camera, his face and body filled out, hair cut short to minimize his male pattern baldness, looking relaxed in a denim shirt. He talked about his quick climb to fame and quicker descent into alcoholism, his new sobriety and the methods he used to centre himself. He had a new acoustic solo album out and a song on the soundtrack of an animated children's film, plans to reunite The Governors General, a boat anchored somewhere in Florida.

"Do you keep in touch with Donna?" the interviewer asked from off-screen.

Mickey paused and scratched at his chin. "Donna is still very much a part of my life. She always will be."

Was that a shadow of regret that passed on Mickey's face during the pause? The interview left her deeply unsatisfied, more confused than anything. Angry. Cinnamon whimpered, and Donna realized how hard she'd been petting her.

The following morning, she sat down at her computer and applied for a distance education course in canine nutrition. In the first name field on the application, she used her full given name, Donna-Marie.

DONNA-MARIE, DRUNK, perches on the lid of a toilet in a stall in the cavernous, white-tiled hotel bathroom across from the ballroom. She feels the air pressure change as someone opens the exterior door, the muffled sound from outside suddenly sharp — the final chorus.

> *D-d-d-d-d-d-do me Donna*
> *Peel me back, like a banana*
> *God-d-d-damn, just do me Donna*

I need it, I can't live without ya

The song is muted again, replaced by heels on tile and a woman's voice: "Donna-Marie, honey, you in here? I've got your shoes."

"D-d-Donna-Marie?" another female voice says, slurring. "D-d-d—"

The first woman stifles a laugh. "Shush, you."

Donna-Marie leans her back into the sweating toilet tank, lifts her soggy feet off the floor, and braces them against the stall door. The heeled feet clack around for a few more seconds—the women whisper-shouting her name—before the door opens to the roar of the dancers. The crowd has moved on to a new song.

When the door swings shut and the room goes quiet, she drops her feet back to the ground and lurches upright. The movement does a number on her stomach and bile climbs into her throat. She flips around to lean over the toilet, her hair dipping into the water. Donna-Marie, knees bent, wrists twisted against the stall walls.

THE LAST TIME DONNA-MARIE sees Mickey on the television will be a few days shy of her sixty-third birthday. She'll be sitting upright in bed, computer open on her lap as she confirms an order from a major natural-foods grocery

chain, her breakfast smoothie leaving a ring on the nightstand as it sweats. Pistachio, her Corgi, will be snoring on
a mat on the floor, Hooch curled into the side of her calf
on top of the duvet, drool gathering in his greying muzzle,
TV playing from the dresser across from her, national news
on low. Downstairs, Gord will swear intermittently as he
tries to inset a leaf into their dining table in preparation for
Donna-Marie's birthday dinner. When she sees Mickey's
face, Donna-Marie will notch the volume up to drown out
the sound of her neighbour's leaf blower, of Gord's curs-
ing. The coroner's report will confirm renal failure after a
lengthy illness, and the montage will cover both the band
and the solo years but be heavy on the early days. Donna-
Marie's eyes will drift momentarily from the television to
the mirror beside it, and she'll watch as her hand floats up
across her chest to grasp the opposite shoulder, holding
herself, and she will feel sad, really and truly gutted by
the news, in a way that is both complex and simple all at
once. When the newscaster states that, while Mickey "had
a career nearly four decades long, he failed to recapture
the magic of his breakthrough single," Donna-Marie will
surprise herself by feeling deeply embarrassed for Mickey,
at his desire for attention, at his need for her specifically
to see him. A message notification from her production
manager will chime on her computer, but she will ignore
it and close the screen, and when the song's chorus comes

on to segue into the sports highlights, Donna-Marie won't turn the sound down but will close her eyes for a moment. Downstairs, Gord will call up to her, something indiscernible about tablecloths. The condensation from the smoothie glass will begin to pool, and a drop will fall from the corner of the nightstand. Outside, the leaf blower will continue to drone. On the bed, Hooch will roll over and whimper in his sleep and kick out his hind feet as though being pursued or maybe in pursuit of something, and Donna-Marie will instinctively reach out, rub his belly until he calms.

Acknowledgements

Thank you to Joshua Greenspon, Zoe Kelsey, Debby de Groot, Tilman Lewis, Lucia Kim, and everyone at House of Anansi Press for giving this book a better home than I'd dreamed of.

Thank you to my editor, Sanchari Sur, for the guidance and support, and for pushing without shoving.

Thank you to Andy Verboom and Kailie Wakeman for the cover art, and for getting the ball rolling.

Thank you to all the editors and publications that have given my work a place to live. Earlier versions of stories in this book first appeared in *Maisonneuve*, *EVENT*, the *Literary Review*, *Going Down Swinging*, *Isthmus Review*, *Humber Literary Review*, *Nashwaak Review*, the *Feathertale Review*, *Riddle Fence*, the *Canary Press*, *Grain*, *adda*, and *Little Fiction*'s *A Mixtape of Words* anthology.

Thank you to the University of British Columbia's Creative Writing Program and to those whose notes scribbled in the margins helped shape my storytelling: Nancy Lee, Keith Maillard, Ian Williams, John Vigna, and Maureen Medved. Thank you to Ramon Kubicek at Langara College for nudging me in the right direction.

Thank you to the friends and colleagues who shelled out advice in coffee shops and living rooms: Adrick Brock, Curtis LeBlanc, Dominique Bernier-Cormier, Kate Balfour, Laura Trethewey, Mallory Tater, Adam Hill, and Shaun Robinson. A huge additional thanks to Jen Neale and Karina Palmitesta for their editing prowess and for never telling me what I wanted to hear.

Thank you to Carleigh Baker, John Elizabeth Stintzi, Michael Melgaard, Jessica Westhead, and again to Jen and Nancy for your generous words. I admire you all.

Thank you to my parents, Dan and Laureen Evans, for instilling in me a lifelong love of books. Thanks for quietly turning pages with me.

Most of all, thank you, Rachel, for giving me room to breathe and a kick in the pants, and Helen, for helping me learn how to learn again.